RED

London Buses at the Front

Blood on the Killing Fields

Poppies

Table of Contents

Red Lights on the Somme

Virgin Soldiers

Chapter 1

The young Lieutenant lay in the big brass bed, he had been a virgin less than an hour ago; the young French woman lying beside him was naked. He looked at her. She was exquisite, perfect breasts not large, not small, just perfect. Her white skin, her red hair all combined to create an image from paradise.

He had visited this establishment on the recommendation of his friend and comrade, Lieutenant Geoffrey Baxter. It was called "Maison de Plaisirs".

She whispered.

'Mon Ami, you must go now… there are more waiting.

'I understand.'

He got up off the bed and slowly dressed into his uniform. He turned around and kissed her gently on the lips.

'I will be back when I am next on leave.'

She simply nodded and showed him the door.

As he departed he looked down the wide stairs to view a number of officers sitting in lounge seats in front of a roaring fire, drinking scotch and patiently waiting.

This was completely different from the red light establishment located in the next street where the enlisted men sought their carnal pleasures.

The young Lieutenant's name was Lawrence Greythorn; he had been commissioned only six months prior after graduating from the officers' training academy at Trinity College, Cambridge. The year was 1916; he had turned eighteen on the eleventh of June.

Lawrence had seen action only once so far, at Fromelles in Northern France not far from Poperinge the town where "Maison de Plaisirs" was located.

It was there where Lawrence had witnessed "hell on earth" and he had made a pledge to himself while lying in a German shell hole: 'Lawrence, you will not die a virgin'. He had just fulfilled that pledge.

Strolling through the streets of Poperinge, still feeling a warm glow, he thought back on his experiences only five days before.

He had been sitting in a hastily dug trench with his men waiting for the signal which would send these young warriors over the top, to what, he didn't know. No-man's land stretched more than four hundred metres and the Germans had been entrenched for over two years. They would be well prepared to receive the Commonwealth troops comprising British and Australians. Most of them would be inexperienced and young.

The British artillery had been blasting the Germans for the past seven hours and the senior officers assured their troops the Krauts would be decimated; they'd hardly put up a fight, they boasted.

The five-minute whistle sounded and Lawrence reminded his platoon to ensure their bayonets were properly fixed and their hand grenades were fastened to their belts.

The attack whistle sounded. He ordered his men to quickly climb the ladders and clamber over the parapet and run as fast as they could. This order was unlike the orders given at The Somme where the officers were instructed by their Generals to walk slowly and deliberately towards the German defences. The result of this ridiculous instruction was twenty thousand dead and forty thousand wounded and missing on the first day of the battle.

Finally, when the last of his men had departed the trench, Lawrence climbed the ladder making his way into no-man's land. It was horrendous; by the time he had progressed less than ten yards, he counted twenty of his men down. Some he recognised, most he didn't, as their facial features had been completely destroyed. He continued on his way through the mud and slime and the lifeless soldiers, some already being devoured by the ubiquitous rats. The noise was immense, with guns, artillery and screaming from both sides.

Lawrence has been ordered to help take the enormous gun emplacement the boys had nicknamed "sugar loaf". They were fighting beside the Australian 59th Division who were as raw as his own troops.

The Germans were well and truly ready, having survived the artillery bombardment that Haig, the British General, threw at them. The Boche simply hunkered down in their deep reinforced bunkers and waited for the shells to stop. The eerie silence was their signal to man their trenches ready to greet the enemy forces. They certainly greeted them with a barrage of machine gun fire and intense shelling. The end result was over five thousand Australian casualties and over fifteen hundred British troops lost their lives in a single day.

Lieutenant Lawrence Greythorn was one of the survivors with no physical injuries but mental scars he would never be able to heal.

Bawdy Behaviour

Chapter 2

Harold Andersen was a fun-loving scoundrel from East London, who liked nothing better than to play football for his beloved "Redbridge Football Club" on weekends and getting pissed with his team-mates after the game, win, lose or draw.

During the week he worked at the Vauxhall Motor Company as a fitter and turner.

He caught the number 67 bus and always sat upstairs if there was room. He enjoyed the view and the fresh air, come rain or shine.

1916 East London

Harry's life was about to change; he had been excused from enlisting when Britain declared war against Germany in 1914. Harry's trade and the industry he worked in meant he was not permitted to sign up for the great adventure. He was needed to help manufacture tanks and other forms of military vehicles for the war effort. Most of his footy mates had joined the army and a few had already lost their lives fighting for King and country.

The Battle of The Somme had proved a disaster for Britain which had lost six hundred and twenty-four thousand of their finest young men.

The army needed to replace them if they were to win the war. Harry's status changed, he was permitted to enlist and did so immediately.

After six weeks of military training he was shipped off to France to join the fray.

HMAT Ascanius

They loaded the troops on board the "Ascanius" as though they were cattle. Every spare foot was utilized for the short trip to Marseilles. The task of finding the toilet proved too difficult for Harry, so he and his mates simply "did their business" over the side.

Harry was well pleased to berth at Marseilles and breathe some clean air; on board was stifling.

At least he had six or seven mates with him from his neighbourhood, all with the same desire to kill some Germans and hopefully meet some pretty French girls. Seeing a bit of France at the same time was a bonus.

The only thing Harry knew about France was they ate frogs, drank wine and beheaded all the rich bastards in the French Revolution.

His mates probably knew even less.

They were herded into a train and transported from the bottom of France up to the very top: Lille.

The conversation on the train varied from 'I wonder what war will be like' to 'I wonder where I can meet a French girl'.

Harry was reticent.

'I think it's going to be tough, bullets and shells flying everywhere and from the newspaper reports I read back home, a lot of us are going to get killed.'

'It won't be us,' said his best mate, Dave Hailes. 'We're too tough and too smart to cop a bullet. Don't worry, Harry, she'll be right. We'll all stick together and beat the shit out of the fucking Krauts.'

'Yeah, that's right Dave, we'll fucking kill them… literally.' Robbie Hall, the eldest of the group, exclaimed.

The other topic of conversation related to how they were going to get shagged.

'I reckon our best bet is to visit one of them knocking shops. They're in every bloody village, so I hear'. Robbie explained.

'All right, you blokes, who hasn't had a naughty yet?'

The men all looked at each other; none was going to admit to being a virgin.

'Geez Robbie, give a bloke a bit of respect why don't you?' complained Willie, the youngest in the group.

'Alright, alright, don't get all funny with me. Just saying that if you want some advice, you can come to me. I am a very experienced bloke when it comes to matters of hanky panky.'

'Thanks, Robbie, but we are experienced men here. We know what's what in relation to all of that,' said Dave.

'Ok. Just asking.'

The troops were given three days' leave when they arrived in Lille so they would be happy and fresh for the coming battles.

They all decided to head for the village of Poperinge just forty-five kilometres from Lille. Poperinge had the reputation of a town where anything goes and it usually did.

Poperinge 1914-1918

Located in the West Flanders region of Belgium, near to the border with France, Poperinge was just behind Allied lines and served as a R&R spot for Allied troops. Allied soldiers knew the town as "Pops". Most of the British soldiers who fought on the Western Front passed through Poperinge. The town served as a major British supply base and garrison for the front.

Poperinge also became the hub for informal social life for Allied soldiers, particularly British troops, during the war. "Pops" provided soldiers with a brief reprieve from the harsh life of the trenches and the front. A thriving black market trade developed, with British military supplies being sold at inflated prices. The town also had numerous cafés, estaminets (bars or pubs) and brothels, which were frequented by the troops. Poperinge was a safe place for British troops and supply depots because it lay just beyond the range of German artillery.

Talbot House:

One of the centres of social life for soldiers in Poperinge during the First World War was Talbot House. Talbot House was established in 1915 as a club for

British soldiers by Reverend Philip "Tubby" Clayton and Chaplain Neville Talbot. Talbot House was named for Chaplain Talbot's younger brother, Lieutenant Gilbert Talbot, who had recently been killed in the vicinity of the nearby villages of Hooge and Zillebeke.

Reverend "Tubby" Clayton was a short thirty-year old vicar in the Anglican Church. He had arrived in Belgium in November 1915 and was assigned to serve as the military chaplain to the British 16th Infantry Brigade. The previous chaplain for the 16th Brigade had been killed the month before.

When Reverend Clayton visited Poperinge he observed that aside from cafés, drinking spots, and houses of prostitution, soldiers had no places to go in the town. Clayton wanted to establish a place for soldiers to gather that was removed from the 'debauchery' that characterized many of the other places that British soldiers frequented.

A British Soldier's Sketch of Talbot House

'Right, lads,' said Robbie as they entered the town, 'Everyman for himself. You can pop into Talbot House and have a nice cup of tea or you can come with me to a bawdy house.'

The soldiers looked at each other, waiting for one of them to take the lead. Finally Harry muttered

'I didn't come here to die a virgin. There, now you know I have never been with a woman and that's about to bloody change. I'm with you, Robbie, lead the way.'

The other young soldiers without admitting to their own virginity agreed to go with Robbie.

They all sauntered along the narrow streets of "Pops" until they spotted a red light outside a four-storey terrace building. Judging by the noise emanating from inside house they thought they had found the right place. The shingle beside the door read "Maison de Plaisirs" they knew they had found the right place.

Robbie instructed the group to wait outside while he entered the establishment to determine its suitability. He spoke to a very attractive mature woman at reception, who was known as Madame Fifi.

'Mademoiselle, I have six virgin soldiers waiting outside, all very keen to have their first…experience. Would you recommend any particular ladies who could teach them the joys of sex?'

'Monsieur, all our ladies would be suitable. Half the young soldiers who visit Maison de Plaisir for the first time are virgins; they are just boys when they enter and men when they leave. If they survive the next few weeks of fighting, they come back,'

'OK, that sounds great. Could I ask the price please?'

'The rate is 2.5 francs for thirty minutes. May I suggest if these boys are not experienced they should book one hour so they are not… how should I say it not hurried. '

'That seems reasonable; I'll go and get them. Is there much of a wait Madame?

'About an hour or so... my girls are very popular.'

Robbie went out side to find the lads in a circle, hands in their pockets looking very nervous.

'Right, lads, it's all sorted, you get one hour with the young lady and it will set you back five francs.

'Bloody hell! Five francs? That's a lot of coin to put up,' complained Dave. 'It better be bloody worth it.'

'You can pull out Dave, if ya like. What about the rest of you?'

The other soldiers looked at each other and in turn agreed to go in. Dave joined them.

'Right, let's get going.'

Robbie led the young band in and they paid their five francs over to Madam Fifi.

'You are a fine looking group I'm sure my girls will like you. I will give you a room number, and then just enter through that door to the waiting area.'

They all moved on to the so-called waiting area. The sight that confronted them was a staircase leading up to all the levels of the house. On every step was a soldier from Britain, France, Canada, Australia and New Zealand all talking and laughing and waiting their turn.

The boys from East London started to talk amongst themselves and shared a few jokes with the Aussies above them on the staircase. Even though they seemed relaxed they were all very nervous except for Robbie who was an old hand at this sort of thing.

They gradually moved up the stairs as the soldiers before them left the premises after their thirty minutes of pleasure.

Dave was the first in the group to reach the first floor landing where their allocated rooms were located. A mature rather buxom Mademoiselle beckoned him to follow her into a small alcove. Dave hoped this was not his lady for the night so to speak; she wasn't; her job was to get him ready to enter the boudoir of the young prostitute. She got down on her knees unbuttoned his fly and sucked him until he thought he would burst. She then opened the door for him and he entered a warm room with many soft furnishings. Reclined on the bed was a pretty young thing no more than eighteen with dark hair and large breasts. Her skin was milky white and she looked absolutely inviting.

She smiled and said 'Bonsoir, cheri.'.

Dave understood enough French to know she had greeted him warmly.

'What is your name, Darlin?'

'Je m'appelle Cloé.'

'Well, Cloé, it is lovely to meet you.'

'Now, I take it you would like me to undress and get into bed with you?'

'Oui'

Dave did as instructed and Cloé proceeded to lick his ear while stroking his still hard cock.

She then straddled him and slowly sat on his magnificent weapon!

Dave had only dreamed of such lovemaking and soon learnt a number of positions he knew nothing of before entering the bedroom. Fifteen minutes later he exploded.

Cloé let him calm down for a little while and then sucked him hard again and repeated the performance. In the hour Dave had paid for, he had gone from virgin soldier to ejaculating three times.

He left the room and walked down the stairs as if in a dream, not noticing who was around him including a couple of his good mates.

The plan was to meet at the Hotel Recours after they were all finished.

Dave, being the first cab off the rank, arrived at the little hotel first. It was a very popular watering hole for soldiers of all nationalities and towards the end of the night could become a bit rough.

Dave went to the bar and ordered a pint he looked around to see if he could see anybody he knew.

He sauntered over to the fireplace and leaned against the mantelpiece,where he noticed a soldier from his division, Frank Porter, and he started up a conversation.

'It's a bit chilly out there. Glad the fire is going'.

'I wouldn't know. I've been in here for the last couple of hours so I wouldn't have a clue what's it's like outside. You been somewhere else, have ya?'

'Well, between you and me I've been at "Maison de Plaisir" for the past few hours."

'Have ya now? So you'd be feeling pretty fucking good.'

'I certainly do.'

'Who were ya with then?'

'Cloe... she was fantastic.'

'Geez, mate, you better make sure your dick doesn't drop off ! She's full of the pox.'

'That's bullshit and you know it.'

'I'm telling you, she's a dirty girl. The old tart that runs the place usually palms here off to the virgins! That's it; hey, everybody, Dave here was a fucking virgin until a few hours ago. Guess who he fucked? Cloe!'

The soldiers nearby started laughing and mocking poor Dave. It was too much for him he turned around and hit Frank right square in the face. Frank went down, holding his nose, with blood streaming out between his fingers.

'You broke my bloody nose, you bastard.'

Frank pulled a knife from his belt and stabbed Dave in the chest, not once but at least a dozen times. Dave dropped down to the floor. He didn't move.

He had dreamed of joining the army and fighting for his country and his family back home. He was going to kill Germans and return home a hero and marry his sweetheart, Emma. He didn't envisage he would be murdered by one of his own, defending the honour of a French prostitute.

It didn't take long for the military police to arrive and arrest Frank. The dragged him to the town hall and locked him in a cell in the basement. These cells were used to hold deserters the night before they were tied to the execution post in the courtyard and shot.

The Judge Advocate was called, heard the eyewitness accounts and pronounced the death penalty.

At dawn the next morning Frank was tied up like a sausage a thick bandage was tied around his face. A square piece of material was pinned to his uniform directly over his heart; that would be the shooter's target.

He was carried by two of the firing squad members into the courtyard and tied to the execution post.

The padre mumbled some words and then went off to have his breakfast.

Two six-strong platoons appeared, lined up with their backs to the firing post. Their guns lay on the ground. The officer gave the signal; they picked up their guns, abruptly turned about, aimed and opened fire. Then they turned their backs on Frank's body and the officer ordered "Quick march!"

The men marched right past Frank, without inspecting their weapons, without turning a head. No military compliments, no parade, no music, no march past; a hideous death, not what he dreamed of when he enlisted to fight for his country.

Behaviour More Refined
Chapter 3

Talbot House was the complete opposite of Maison de Plaisir; it was a place a soldier could go to relax and find peace. Tubby Talbot established "Everyman's Club" to be just that. When a soldier entered Toc H as they all called it, he left his rank at the door; Privates and Captains all interacted and socialized without incident. There were reading rooms and tea-rooms and on the fourth floor Tubby had established a chapel where war-weary soldiers could find some serenity in prayer.

After Dave's murder, the boys all gravitated to Toc H to try and make sense of what had happened. If Dave had died on the battlefield they would raise a glass and toast their friend but cold-hearted murder was a different kettle of fish altogether.

Tubby sat with them and tried to help them understand that Dave was now at peace. They all prayed together and at the end of the night the friends all felt a little better. Wandering back to their barracks the group passed soldiers pissing in the street and laughing and singing bawdy songs. Walking silently, their heads bowed, they ignored their comrades' behaviour.

Toc H became a regular stop for the group when they were on leave although the original band of brothers had been reduced to four. Dave was gone and now Henry and Will had been killed in the battle of Ypres. Will was now out there in no-man's land being eaten by rats or being blown apart by the incessant German shellfire. Henry died as a result of the poison gas, chlorine. His body was retrieved from the trench and given a temporary grave. Unfortunately it was blown away by German shellfire three days later. He is now classified as "Missing".

Gas attack on Gravenstafel

At around 5:00 pm on 22 April 1915, the German Army released one hundred and sixty-eight tons of chlorine gas over a four-mile front on the part of the line held by the Allied troops.

The attack involved a massive logistical effort, as German troops hauled to the front by hand, five thousand seven hundred and thirty cylinders of chlorine gas, weighing ninety pounds each. The Germans relied on the prevailing winds to carry the gas towards enemy lines. This was far from being an accurate method of dispersal and a large number of German soldiers were injured or killed from the gas drifting back onto their lines.

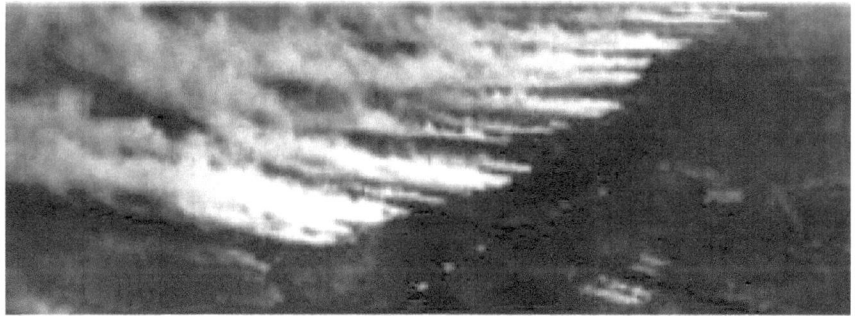

Germans Release Their Gas Attack

Approximately six thousand Allied troops died within ten minutes at Ypres, primarily from asphyxiation and subsequent tissue damage in the lungs. Many more were blinded. Chlorine gas forms Hypochlorous acid and when combined with water, destroys moist tissues such as lungs and eyes. The chlorine gas, being denser than air, quickly filled the trenches, forcing the troops to climb out into heavy enemy fire.

Many of the Allied survivors of the gas attacks abandoned their positions, which created a four-mile gap along the front line.

The German High Command did not anticipate how effective this new weapon would be and did not allocate reserves to take advantage of their strategic win. The Germans waited until dusk before they moved their troops forward.

The Allies were able to counteract the gas by urinating into their hankies and holding it against their faces; the improvised gas masks worked and the Allies were able to hold off the German attacks until 3 May 1915. The cost? Six thousand dead.

Henry Fulton and Will Hadler were good mates from East London, members of the group of mates led by Robbie Hall. They had been transferred to one of General French's Divisions commanded by General Smith-Dorrien. There was no love lost between the two Generals but French was the superior officer and had to be obeyed.

Will and Henry were equipped with gas masks in anticipation of the new weapon of war the Germans were rumoured to unleash.

'These fucking masks are bloody uncomfortable, mate. I'm in half a mind to take the bloody thing off and take my chances.

'Henry, I really don't think that's a very good idea. You take the thing off and you're guaranteed to die a horrible death. They say it's slow and fucking painful. You're better off running into a German bullet. Keep the thing on for God's sake.'

Then they heard the young Lieutenant yell 'GAS' several times. They peered over the escarpment and could see a yellowish cloud rolling towards them.

Henry and Will adjusted their masks to ensure they were nice and tight even if bloody uncomfortable.

The gas was close to hitting the British trenches when quite a few soldiers jumped over the top and started making their way towards Gerry's lines. Will was one of those soldiers. He crouched down making a beeline for the German trenches when suddenly a searing pain shot through his knees and he collapsed down into the bog they called no-man's land. Knowing it would be impossible to get back to his own trench, Will looked around for a shell crater, which would offer some protection from the barrage. The blood was oozing down his leg and when he tried to slither in the mud the pain shot all the way up his body and into his head. Still, he knew he had to get to a crater and hoped the stretcher-bearers would find him and take him back. Painfully, Will slid towards the nearest crater when he heard the sound of a shell. The boys in the trenches often said 'If you can hear the shell above the mayhem of battle, it's yours.' It was Will's; it landed almost directly on the wounded soldier, exploding and spreading his body parts over a wide area. He would never be found.

Henry stayed back in the trench hoping the bloody gas mask would do its job. He and his comrades watched as the deadly cloud approached and rolled over the trench. Henry started to feel a burning pain in his throat and eyes. He started to suffocate. The pain was unbearable in his chest; it felt like he had been stabbed in the sternum. Henry was having trouble breathing and was hyperventilating.

He started to cough uncontrollably and his eyes were stinging like he had never felt before. He vomited and could not stop, but at least the pain was easing. Henry tried to swallow his own spittle but his mouth was dry as and his tongue felt twice its normal size. He felt he had to lie down; the bottom of the trench is where the gas accumulates. Henry gasped in the gas and as he lay there in shocking pain, he drifted into unconsciousness and died. So much for the mask that was meant to save his life.

Passschendaele

Chapter 4

Passchendaele 1917

The Battle of Passchendaele was one of the major battles of the First World War, taking place between July and November 1917. In a series of attacks, troops under British command attacked the German Army. The battle was fought for control of the small village of Passchendaele near the town of Ypres in West Flanders, Belgium. The objective of the offensive according to General Haig was to achieve a breakthrough outflanking the German defences forcing

Germany to withdraw from the Channel Ports housing the infamous U Boat submarines. The French Army been suffering endemic mutinies and it was hoped the Battle of Passchendaele would give them some relief and enable the French to sort out their problems.

The British launched several massive attacks, heavily supported by artillery, aircraft and tanks. Unfortunately the thick mud made it difficult for the tanks to get through. The British, with all their firepower never managed to make a decisive breakthrough against well-entrenched German lines. The battle consisted of a series of 'Bite and Hold' attacks to capture critical terrain and wear down the German army. This continued until relieved by the Canadians who took Passchendaele on 6 November 1917, ending the battle. Although inflicting massive casualties on the Germans, the Allies had captured a mere five miles of new territory at a cost of one hundred and forty thousand lives, a ratio of roughly two inches gained per dead soldier. The Germans recaptured their lost ground, without resistance, five months later during the Battle of the Lys; they lost it again in late September 1918 and never regained it for the remainder of the war.

Jim Daniel and Jack Irvine were members of Robbie Hall's band of brothers, mates forever; they had grieved over Dave's murder together and now they were fighting together and finding themselves crawling through thick mud trying to advance on the German line, knowing their mates were doing the same. Unfortunately they could not see them as the haze from the smoke of the artillery and gunfire hung over no-man's land like a London fog.

Jim was a carpenter by trade, the same as Jesus of Nazareth. Jim couldn't imagine Jesus in these circumstances although he knew the likelihood of his life ending at the age of thirty-three, the same age as Jesus, was pretty high.

There seemed to be a lull in the shelling, so Jim and Jack took the opportunity to light up a smoke. It tasted wonderful and was so good to relax just for a little while.

As they lay in the thick mud enjoying their cigarette they heard the familiar sound of German artillery. The sound of the shell approaching became clearer, that terrifying sound.

'Please God, may this one not be for us.'

It was. The shell exploded between the two close friends, tearing off their limbs and scattering their body parts over a twenty-metre radius.

Another four inches gained and two good young men lost.

Robbie would return to Pops whenever he was granted leave; on occasion he would still visit Maison de Plaisir but for the most part he would head directly for Talbot House. Robbie had been promoted to Second Lieutenant, which would entitle him to visit 'La Poupée' a wonderful club restricted to officers only. He did go one time and enjoyed it but he preferred the company of enlisted men. Harry was still convalescing from his leg wound somewhere away from the line. Robbie wasn't sure exactly where but no doubt he would be returning to the fray. It was only Robbie and Harry left from the original band of seven.

Poperinge

At times there were over five hundred thousand allied soldiers moving through Poperinge in a town normally boasting a population of less than ten thousand. The town was transformed during the war to a supply point and R&R centre for the battle-weary troops. Many new restaurants and clubs were established during this time.

One such famous restaurant was "La Poupée" (The Doll) in Market Square where the Cossey family lived. What was to become the prime attraction of the Western Front had started as a simple shop. The patriarch, Elie Cossey, was a shoemaker by trade while his wife kept a lingerie and haberdashery shop at the same address. Elie was a resourceful entrepreneur. The fact that allied troops were pouring into the town presented a fantastic business opportunity. He knew he was not going to make a killing by making shoes nor his wife by selling lingerie. He completely renovated the shop and created a café. He bought an automated honky-tonk piano and so "La Poupée" was born.

Elie Cossey began rubbing shoulders with both the military hierarchy and local councillors; through these elite contacts he was able to procure spirits, a liquor that was almost unavailable at the time. He wanted to ensure that only the best clientele visited the café. He accomplished this by hanging a sign outside the entrance: "OFFICERS ONLY".

Elie's personality, his wife's magnificent cooking and the abundance of spirits all went to make the cafe a great success. What made it even more successful was his three daughters Martha, Marie-Louise and Eliane. At the outbreak of the war, the girls were 22, 21 and 18 years of age respectively. The youngest was a slender, most attractive red-haired girl, a feature that earned her the nickname of "Ginger". Such was her fame that officers of all nationalities came from miles around to see this stunning continental beauty and her father's establishment soon became known as "Ginger's", instead of "La Poupee".

Edwin Campion Vaughan, a British officer, wrote in his diary: "The two rooms were full of diners but we found a table in the glass-roofed garden. A sweet little eighteen year-old girl came to serve us. I fell a victim at once to her long red hair and flashing smile. When I asked her name, she replied "Gingair" in such a glib way that we both gave a burst of laughter. We had a splendid dinner with several bottles of bubbly, and Ginger hovered delightfully about us."

There were regulars at "La Poupee" as much as there could be regulars with a war going on less than twenty kilometres away. Most of the officers would have three days leave and then return to the mayhem of the trenches. Some would return, many would not.

There was one particular table, table ten which was always reserved between the hours of eight and ten in the evening. Every night a Lieutenant Colonel would arrive and take his place at his reserved table. His name was Alex Brier, a shy man with a strong angular face and a very kind disposition. Only Ginger was permitted to serve him and over the first three months of 1918, Ginger and Alex became very close. The café closed at ten and when they had cleared the tables, Ginger sat with the young officer and talked.

She would talk about her aspirations of becoming an actress in Paris when the war ended and he talked about Cambridge, England where he had lived before the war and where he would practise law after it had ended.

He never spoke about the war or his role in it, she only knew he was on medical leave but never inquired about his injury and he didn't offer an explanation. She was just happy that Alex was on leave for so long and didn't need to return to the front.

Their relationship blossomed right through 1918 and when the 11th of the 11th arrived, they celebrated together along with the rest of Poperinge's population and the thousands of troops who were in town.

Ginger knew in her heart of hearts that the war's end would mean Alex would be dispatched home to England and she may never see him again. He left France on the 16th December 1918. He didn't say goodbye or promise he would return. She was heartbroken.

In the June of 1919, Ginger decided she had to contact Alex and let him know of her true feelings for him. She wrote to the Veteran Affairs Commission explaining her desire to contact Lieutenant Colonel Alex Brier and lied that she was pregnant to him.

Three weeks later, she received a letter advising her that Lieutenant Colonel Alex Brier had been killed in the Battle of Passchendaele on the 28th of July 1917.

She was shocked and angry. How could the Department have got things so wrong? Obviously he was not killed in 1917: she had sat with him at the restaurant every night after she first met him in January 1918.

She wrote back to Veterans Affairs and asked if there had been another Lieutenant Colonel Alex Brier serving in the armed forces. Two weeks later she received another letter assuring her there was only one Lieutenant Colonel Alex Brier serving in the British Army.

So who was this impostor who had won her heart? His name was Lieutenant Colonel Alex Brier.

Passchendaele to Paris

The two Canadian soldiers were walking along duckboards making their way back to their battalion. They had received medical attention resulting from injuries sustained in the previous weeks fighting at Passchendaele. It was raining as usual which made the boards very slippery; Jimmie Henderson was leading the way with Henry Lee following behind. Jimmie slipped, falling into the quagmire and started to sink slowly and was up to his waist before Henry realised what had happened. Henry quickly lay down on the boards and stretched out his rifle for Jimmie to hold onto.

'Jimmie, get hold of the barrel! I'll pull you out.'

'I can't fucking reach it, just six inches more mate… please.'

'I'll try but I'm almost off the boards myself.'

'Jesus mate, I'm sinking! Do something!'

Duckboards at Passchendaele

Finally, Henry was able to reach his good mate and, with an enormous amount of effort, pulled Jimmie up to the point where he could reach the boards. He struggled onto the walkway with Henry pulling him up by his collar. They both lay there exhausted until they heard the sound of German artillery. They struggled to continue their journey back to their Battalion, making it right on dusk. There were to be no attacks that night so the two lads could rest until the next day. The next morning after a hearty breakfast of stale biscuits and tea they were ready to fight another battle.

The next few weeks consisted of painstakingly slow progress, inching their way through the slime, firing at the German positions. The terrain was littered with dead Canadian soldiers who could not be retrieved. Finally on 6 November, 1917, Passchendaele, or what was left of it, was taken.

The Germans suffered over two hundred thousand casualties, while the British forces also suffered over two hundred thousand including sixteen thousand Canadians.

Henry and Jimmie were granted seven days leave along with many other surviving soldiers from the battle of Passchendaele.

They had a choice of either London or Paris, so they chose Paris. The train was certainly not first class travel and they were cramped into a carriage that would normal take forty passengers; there were seventy Canadian Canuks in the carriage all eager to reach their destination.

The train had barely pulled into Gare du Nord when the soldiers alighted and headed for the exit, ready to discover Paris and all its attractions.

Jimmie and Henry headed off to find suitable accommodation and discovered a lovely small hotel in the Marais, The Hotel Gabriel. It was close to the Eiffel Tower and the Louvre, two sites on the top of their list for daytime sightseeing. It was also not far by train to Montmartre where they intended to spend their evenings at establishments such as Moulin Rouge and the famous brothel, Le Chabanais. It was not their intention to come back to the Western Front with any money in their wallets.

The first full day was spent as they had planned before arriving; they climbed the Eiffel Tower and were amazed at the view. They spent hours in the Louvre and the Musée d'Orsay before finding a café across the river in the Latin Quarter.

'I can't believe this mate. Not five weeks ago I was pulling you out of the mud at Passchendaele and here we are sitting in a Parisian café drinking beer and eating fine food instead of the shit we get for rations on the front.'

'I know, it seems crazy. The only downside is we're going to be back on the front fighting some other bloody battle inside a week. Still, we're here now so let's make the most of it.'

They did. That night they made their way to the red light district of Montmartre and bought a couple of tickets to the famous Moulin Rouge. They loved it; the colour, the music and the girls made the show a wonderful spectacle. The next stop was Le Chabanais; they had heard from the officers that this was the establishment to go to and not pick up the clap.

They knocked on the elaborate front door and waited; within a minute, a young girl dressed in an evening gown opened it.

She introduced herself as Rose and asked the two nervous Canadians to follow her to the waiting room.

Waiting Room, Le Chabanais

'Well, mate, this place is a bit flash. Hope the girls live up to the décor.'

'Yeah, I hope we can afford it. How much dosh have you got on ya?'

'Don't worry, I've got plenty! We're just here to have a good time and forget about the fucking war for a while.'

'Yep, you're dead right, Jimmie, can't wait.'

They didn't have to wait long; Rose began introducing the ladies who were available. A procession of voluptuous young woman entered the parlour, introducing themselves to the two eager soldiers. After they introduced themselves they took a seat on one of the Louis XVI chairs or *chaises longues.* Rose approached Jimmie and Henry and asked if they had made their selections; Jimmie chose a blonde girl who looked about thirty, eight years older than he was. He had always fancied himself with an older, more experienced woman. Henry went for a beautiful redhead much younger than Jimmie's choice.

The two women took the boys' hands and led them down a corridor lined with erotic art.

Jimmie's lady was named Françoise; she led him into an elaborate bedroom decorated in what he thought was an eastern theme. He felt like a Maharajah or a prince or similar.

Jimmie's Room

Henry's redhead was Andréa; she led him into a bedroom next to Jimmie's.

    'I hope I don't make too much noise,' he thought.

He couldn't believe his eyes; he'd never seen any room, let alone a bedroom so luxurious.

Henry's Room

Andréa explained a few rules, including the necessity to wear a "capote anglaise" (Englishmen's coat) for health reasons. These conditions determined why Le Chabanais had the reputation as the cleanest establishment in France.

'I have no idea how to put this thing on, Mademoiselle. I have never used one before.'

'Don't worry, mon cheri, I will put it on for you. I swear you won't even know it is on. Now just relax while I undress you.'

Andréa slowly undid his tunic coat and laid it on a chair. Next, she undid his belt and trouser buttons and slid them over his feet and laid them on the chair. By this time it was obvious that young Henry was quite excited and ready for what was ahead.

She finished undressing him and guided him to the exotic bed.

She undressed slowly and provocatively not taking her eyes off him nor his erection.

Her experience now came to the fore, while performing fellatio she slid the condom on with her lips. She was right; he didn't feel the 'Englishman's overcoat' going on.

She straddled him and for the next sixty minutes, he experienced lovemaking like he had never dreamed of.

At the end of the blissful hour, Henry dressed and kissed Andréa goodbye, promising to return.

He met Jimmie in the reception room. He looked happy, and they both walked out into the street and started to laugh.

'How good was that, Jimmie?'

'If the Krauts shoot me tomorrow, I'll die a happy man.'

'Me too. When are we going back there?'

'Well, I reckon we've got enough dough for one more visit. When you work it out, it costs five francs in Pops for an hour and we just spent fifteen.'

'Yeah, I suppose you're right. We need some money to buy meals and pay the hotel bill.'

The two very content soldiers made their way back to the Marais and retired to their rooms. They both slept very well.

True to their word, Jimmie and Henry returned for a final visit to Le Chabanais. The second time was just as good, albeit with two different ladies.

Finally, and all too quickly, their time in Paris came to an end. They boarded the train to take them north at Gare du Nord railway station. They arrived in Ypres, or what remained of Ypres, on the 18 November 1917.

The two Canuks settled back into the Western Front way of life, hoping there would not be a fourth battle of Ypres. They had had more than their fair share of Passchendaele with its thick slimy mud. They needn't have worried; their next battle would be Cambrai.

The Streets of Cambrai

Bring in the Tanks

Chapter 5

The Battle of Cambrai was fought between 20 November - 7 December 1917. It was the first large scale tank battle in history. It was launched after the failure of the main British autumn offensive of 1917, the Third Battle of Ypres, famous for the Passchendaele mud. It was the mud that had precluded the use of the Tank Corps, which, by November, could field over three hundred tanks.

Brigadier General H. Elles, the commander of the Tank Corps, developed the overall battle plan. His idea was to launch a mass tank attack across the dry chalky ground at Cambrai, where his tanks wouldn't run the risk of bogging down in the mud. General Sir Julian Byng, the Canadian commander of the Third Army, received his plan with some enthusiasm.

The Canadian artillery men had conceived a plan that combined a tank attack with a new type of artillery bombardment that did not require lengthy preparation. Previous bombardments had required a preliminary period of "registration" in which each of the gun batteries had fired practice rounds to determine where their shots were landing.
This alerted the defenders to the possibility of an assault and allowed them to gather reserves.
Brigadier General H.H. Tudor had devised a system to register guns electronically, thus avoiding the need for a long period of preparation.

The battle was to be initiated by over three hundred tanks, spread over a ten kilometre front; they were to be supported by eight infantry divisions. The infantry were to advance close behind the tanks to provide close support. The artillery bombardment would start on the day of the attack, giving no warning of the upcoming assault.

Jimmie and Henry and the rest of their battalion were ordered to fall in behind the tanks. They had been told to stay behind the tanks and use them as protection as they advanced on the enemy.

'What do you think about this, mate? It's a bit different from crawling on your belly through the fucking mud, hey?'

'Yeah, sure is! Those big mothers should stop a few bullets.'

The artillery bombardment began at 6.20 am on 20 November 1917. The two German divisions at Cambrai, the 20th Landwehr and 54th Reserve divisions were caught entirely by surprise. Along most of the line, the British tanks crawled their way through the German wire, across the trenches, and with close infantry support, reached as far as four miles into the German lines.

Things were not going as well in the centre of the British line. The commander of the German 54th Reserve division had prepared anti-tank tactics based around the use of artillery against slowly moving targets i.e. tanks. The infantry of the 51st Highland Division was too far behind the tanks, leaving them vulnerable. Eleven were destroyed in front of the advancing Highlanders. At the end of the first day the British had created a six-mile wide gap in the German lines, but with a salient at its centre.

The allied success at Cambrai on 20 November was treated as a great victory in Britain; the church bells rang out for the first time since 1914. However, after their initial success the advance slowed down. The tanks of 1917 were still not mechanically reliable and many had broken down under the stresses of the advance. Some limited progress was made over the next week, but the defences of the Hindenberg line held.

While the British were inching their way forward, the Germans were preparing for a counterattack.

On 30 November, twenty German divisions under the command of Crown Prince Rupprecht and General von Marwitz launched a massive counterattack that forced the British out of many of the areas they had captured on 20 November and even captured some areas held by the British before the start of the battle. On 4 December, General Haig ordered a withdrawal from much of the remaining salient to shorten the lines. The battle, which had started with such a dramatic breakthrough ended with the restoration of the status quo.

Jubilant Canadians at Cambrai

Losses were roughly equivalent on both sides. The British lost forty three thousand men, many during the German counterattack. Germans losses were similar, between forty and fifty thousand men. The main achievement of the British Tank Corps at Cambrai was to demonstrate all too clearly the potential of the tank. The German tank programme was perhaps their biggest failure of the war. In the crucial battles of 1918, the Germans would have to rely on captured British and French tanks and a very small number of their own inefficient and ineffective A7V tanks.

Jimmie survived Cambrai; Henry did not. He has never been found.

Ole Bill Joins the War

Chapter 6

Ole Bill

Harry was due to be picked up from Poperinge with his Company; they were to be transported to Ypres. His first time in Ypres was unforgettable; he fought in the Battle for Passchendaele where two of his good mates, Henry and Will lost their lives.

He hoped that their remains would be found eventually and he would be able to visit their graves. Currently they were lost in the muddy slime of what was no-man's land.

They had been waiting for about an hour when Robbie pointed down the road.

'Will you have a look at what they have sent us to get back to the front? Fucking London buses!'

'They're still painted red, for God's sake. They'll make a nice target for the Krauts,' Harry retorted.

The buses pulled up at the collection point and the soldiers began to board. Harry started to laugh.

'I don't fucking believe it! This is the bus I used to catch to go to work back home.'

'No, pull the other one, Harry,' Robbie sniggered.

'I'm telling you, it's my old bus, number 67. Warren Stackhouse was our driver.'

Harry started to board "Ole Bill" as the buses were called when he stopped and started to laugh again.

'Well, this beats it all! Warren Fucking Stackhouse. How are you, you old bastard?'

'Harry, my boy, you've managed to keep your head on, I see.'

'Yeah, so far. How did you get roped into this?

'When they seconded all the buses I didn't have a job, so I thought fuck it, I may as well join.'

Harry and his mates were ready to ride off to Ypres in the number 67 bus with Wazza driving. Just like home except he was going into battle and not to work.

'Come on, Robbie, let's get upstairs; that's where I always used to sit.'

'Yeah, alright; we should make a nice target for a Kraut plane up there. Come on, what the fuck.'

The two soldiers clambered up the spiral steps with their full packs and rifles, getting stuck every now and then but eventually making it.

Ole Bill began its arduous journey along the dirt road covered in potholes and dangerous embankments. Robbie and Harry were taking in the scenery, which was largely pristine, untouched by battle. The sky was clear, perfect for flying and that's what the German pilot thought when he spotted the convoy of buses heading for the front.

He flew down low and dropped a bomb; it hit bus 67 right on the driver's cabin. Wazza Stackhouse was killed instantly. The bus ploughed down the embankment, rolling over on its side. Ironically only two other soldiers were killed; the remainder survived with relatively minor injuries, including Robbie and Harry.

The surviving soldiers were picked up three hours later and continued their journey to Ypres.

Other vehicles used in the war included The Rolls Royce "Silver Ghost"

OORLOG 1914-1915 — POPERINGHE. • Engelsche troepen op de Londensche Autobussen ingebracht.
Troupes anglaises emmenées sur les Autobus Londoniens.
British troops brought in London autobusses.

Visé, Paris N° 42

UITGEVER-Sansen Vannesten, Poperinghe

Buses Loaded With Troops Heading for Ypres

They Don't Shoot Officers: Do They?

Chapter 7

Western Front, France, January 1917

Lieutenant Lawrence Greythorn had within the first twelve months of arriving in France lost his virginity and fought in two major battles including the Battle of Fromelles. He had come of age although still only nineteen, turning twenty in March.

The trenches with their confined spaces and constant dampness, not to mention rats and stinking latrines were not a place he really wanted to be but as an officer of the British Army he didn't have to share this stinking environment.

At least Lawrence was housed in the "officers' quarters" which had some home comforts and while they waited for the call to attack, they could enjoy a nice cup of tea.

Officer's Quarters Western Front

The troops had no such luxuries. They waited in the trenches, either freezing cold or oppressively hot, depending on the season.

Young Lawrence had been acting a little strangely since he last led his men into battle. He was normally a gregarious sort of a person but lately he had withdrawn into himself. The other officers, including his commanding officer, Captain Terrence Kirby, were aware of the change but put it down to tiredness and homesickness.

Orders came through from Military High Command that an offensive against the German lines would commence at 5am on 28th of January.

All the officers met and discussed the order and the tactics they would employ. MHC had promised them eight hours of artillery bombardment starting at 9pm that night.

These were the same tactics the British had used since the beginning of the war. The formula for attacking German lines was 50 to 1; that is for every fifty

British and Commonwealth soldiers killed, one German would die. The odds were not good.

Lieutenant's Greythorn platoon was now a well -seasoned group of fighting men, although many of the original group were no longer with them and replacements had made up the numbers.

The men were waiting silently for the whistle signalling them to go over the top; some prayed, some wrote a note to their loved ones and stuck it onto the sand bags and others just waited silently.

Lieutenant Greythorn was checking his fob watch. When five o'clock came, he blew the whistle and his men climbed the ladders and started to run as best they could, in the pock- marked landscape towards the German lines.

When the last man had left the trench, young Lawrence could not move; as much as he willed himself to climb the ladder, he froze. He collapsed to the floor of the trench and sobbed, lying in a foetal position. This is how Captain Kirby found him.

'Greythorn, what in the hell do you think you're doing, man?

Get up and join your men, you bloody coward!'

Greythorn did not even look up at his commanding officer.

'I'm warning you, if you don't get up and climb that ladder, I'll

have you court-martialled and shot!'

Lawrence could do nothing. He had entered a world where he had not been before. He could hear Captain Kirby but it was as though Kirby was far away in the distance.

'Right, stay here.'

Lawrence wasn't going anywhere; he couldn't move, even if he wanted to.

Captain Kirby returned a few minutes later, accompanied by two armed soldiers who dragged Lawrence away and shoved him into a dug-out and locked the door.

The young Lieutenant was immersed in grief. He had dreamed of the day he would join the army and become an officer like his father and grandfather before him. He could not understand what had happened: one minute he was ordering his men to climb the ladders and the next, he was a quivering mess on the bottom of the trench.

His career as an officer was effectively over and his future was uncertain. He could well be shot for cowardice and disobeying an order from a superior officer. He lay in the dimly lit dug-out for what seemed like days but in fact was eight hours. The noise of battle had ceased and he could hear troops moving about in the trenches. Suddenly the door was opened and he was ordered out, two military policemen grabbed him and he was escorted through the trench to the exit sap where he was loaded onto a military bus for transportation to Armentieres where he would be held in a prison cell until his court-martial. The men in the trenches just stared at him. He had been an officer , well-liked and respected by the men, but now he was just another coward.

Lawrence did not attempt to speak to his two-man guard on the three-hour trip to Armentieres; he just hung his head and wondered what lay ahead.

The bus arrived at three o'clock and Lawrence was escorted into the prison and placed in a cell. It was very spartan with a bunk bed and a bucket in the corner. This was to be his home for the next month or so.

The first night in the cell was a cathartic experience for young Lawrence. He thought about his home in Essex, England and his family. He knew his father would disown him. His only son being court martialled would be almost too much for the retired Major.

Breakfast was served at seven am if you could call it breakfast - some type of gruel and a mug of cold weak tea. The guard, Horace, assigned to him, was quite a friendly chap and after a while they started to have conversations about anything but the war.

One day Horace looked in on Lawrence and noticed he looked particularly glum.

'What's up, Lawrence? You don't look too happy today.'

'I am just sad that my family will have to live with the fact that I was executed in disgrace. They should have been proud of me, not ashamed of me.

'Well, for a start, Gov, they haven't executed any officers since I've been here... plenty of privates but no officers.'

'I think I would rather be shot than go home in disgrace and be placed in a civilian prison for God knows how long.'

'I bet you would change your mind if you were tied to the execution post with a dozen rifles pointed at you!'

'Maybe; I don't know.

Greythorn's Cell

Let's Even Up the Score

Chapter 8

1916 December France

Several officers were briefing Field Marshal Sir Douglas Haig, in his château some distance from the British front line.

General Haig's Château

The briefing concentrated on the number of deserters and soldiers displaying cowardice and being executed. The officers thought it was having an adverse effect on general troop morale.

In 1916 alone, nearly one hundred British and Commonwealth soldiers had been executed. The only country which would not allow executions was Australia.

In total, throughout World War One, there were three hundred and six British and Commonwealth soldiers executed. The executions, primarily of non-commissioned ranks, included twenty-five Canadians, twenty-two Irishmen and five New Zealanders.

Between 1914 and 1918, the British Army identified eighty thousand men with shellshock. Most could not stand the thought of being on the front line any longer and deserted. Once caught, they received a court martial and, if sentenced to death, were shot by a twelve man firing squad.

The horrors that men from all sides endured while on the front line cannot be imagined.

"We went up into the front line near Arras, through sodden and devastated countryside. As we were moving up to our sector along the communication trenches, a shell burst ahead of me and one of my platoon dropped. He was the first man I ever saw killed. Both his legs were blown off and the whole of his body and face was peppered with shrapnel. The sight turned my stomach. I was sick and terrified but even more frightened of showing it." (Victor Silvester)

Haig and his senior military commanders would not accept that a soldier's failure to return to the front line was anything other than desertion. They also believed that if such behaviour was not harshly punished, others might be encouraged to do the same and the whole discipline of the British Army would collapse. Some men faced a court martial for other offences but the majority stood trial for desertion from their post; "fleeing in the face of the enemy". A court martial itself was usually carried out with some speed and the execution followed shortly after.

Few soldiers wanted to be in a firing squad. Many were soldiers at a base camp recovering from wounds that still stopped them from fighting at the front but did not preclude them from firing a Lee Enfield rifle. Some of those in firing squads were under the age of sixteen, as were some of those who were shot for 'cowardice'. James Crozier from Belfast was shot at dawn for desertion; he was just sixteen. Before his execution, Crozier was given so much rum that he passed out. He had to be carried, semi-conscious, to the place of execution. Officers at the execution later claimed that there was a very real fear that the men in the firing squad would disobey the order to shoot. Private Abe Bevistein, aged sixteen, was also shot by firing squad at Labourse, near Calais. As with so many others cases, he had been found guilty of deserting his post.

'Well, what do you expect me to do? Pardon all these bastards and send them home to their mummies?' Haig sneered.

'No, Sir, but I think if we demonstrated to the troops we were not being elitist and began executing a few officers, we might lift the men's spirits a tad,' suggested General Haker.

'How many officers have we tried and found guilty, General?'

'I think it is in the range of six, Sir.'

'Well, pull a couple out and go and shoot them, for God's sake.'

'How do we choose which two, Sir?

'I don't care who you bloody choose; get them to pick straws or some bloody thing. Just do it and do it tomorrow at dawn. Is that clear?'

'I take it, General, that's an order?'

'Yes, that's a bloody order.'

'Now if that is all we have to discuss I am going to have my lunch.'

The Last Dawn

Chapter 9

Lieutenant Lawrence Greythorn was reading *Great Expectations* by Charles Dickens when an officer entered his cell. He had not met Captain Napier before.

'Lieutenant Lawrence Greythorn, you have been found guilty of cowardice by the authorised court and have been sentenced to death. You will be taken to a place of execution tomorrow morning where you will be shot by a firing squad at dawn. Do you have any questions?'

'No Sir.'

Captain Napier did not salute; he about faced and exited the cell, leaving Lawrence to contemplate his fate.

Lawrence surprised himself by returning to chapter thirteen of his book. He read until lights out at ten thirty.

He didn't sleep much that night.

Greythorn was woken at five am and offered breakfast. No special breakfast, just the same old stuff: so much for the condemned man's last meal.

At five thirty, his escort arrived. They manacled his writs and attached leg irons to his ankles and helped him hobble to the courtyard only thirty metres away. The two soldiers tied him to the execution pole. Captain Napier entered the courtyard and pinned a white handkerchief to his uniform about where his heart was located; they then placed a hood over his head.

He could hear the execution party marching out and knew his time on this earth had just about come to an end.

The execution party faced away from the young Lieutenant and when given the order, they picked up their rifles from the cobblestones, turned, took aim and fired.

Lawrence slumped down; Captain Napier walked over, removed the hood and decided a bullet to the head was required.

A cart entered the courtyard, loaded up the young warrior and took him away for burial.

During the Great War of 1914-1918 many millions of men lost their lives in one of the greatest acts of barbarity and futility the world has ever seen.

The heroism and sacrifice of troops in the trenches is without parallel. However, during the war, three hundred and six British and Commonwealth soldiers were shot on the orders of the military hierarchy and senior officers. In contrast, the Germans only executed twenty-five of their own. The Australians executed none of their soldiers.

The common theme for justifying the execution of British and Commonwealth soldiers was cowardice: many were suffering from shell shock (also called "war neurosis") and most were deliberately picked out and convicted "as a lesson to others". Other charges carrying the death penalty included desertion and insubordination. Some were simply obeying orders to carry information from one trench to another. Most of those shot were young, defenceless and vulnerable teenagers who had volunteered for duty. They were selected, charged, and subjected to a kangaroo trial often without defence representation. The modus operandi was that they were convicted one day, then shot at dawn the following day. Eyewitness accounts suggest many faced their death with a gallantry absent in their accusers.

General Haig, when questioned, declared that all men accused of cowardice and desertion were examined by a Medical Officer (MO) and that no soldier was sentenced to death if there was any suspicion of him suffering shell shock. The Under-Secretary of State for War also and repeatedly misled the House of Commons on this matter. In fact, most soldiers accused of cowardice and desertion were not examined by an MO, and in the few cases where a medical diagnosis of shell shock had been made, the medical evidence was ignored and the man was convicted and shot regardless. General Haig not only signed all the death warrants but when questioned later on this issue, lied repeatedly. General Haig's behaviour in choosing to murder his own men places him in the category of war criminal. He was in fact, rewarded with the title, "Earl Haig" in 1919.

Spring Time on the Western Front

Chapter 10

March 1918

Robbie Hall and Harry Andersen were the only two left of the original "Band of Brothers" that had arrived in France in the summer of 1916 full of hope and bravado. Harry's leg had completely healed but he still felt twinges of pain particularly when it rained.

They were located south west of a place they had never heard of before the war, Saint Quentin, France.

Saint Quentin was founded by the Romans; it received the name of "Augusta of the Viromandui" in honour of the Emperor Augustus. It is located on the Somme River.

During the early Middle Ages, a major monastery developed, based on pilgrimage to the tomb of Quentin, a Roman Christian who came to evangelise the region and was martyred in Augusta, giving rise to a new town which was named after him.

The city grew rapidly: the "bourgeois" obtained, in the second half of the 11th century a municipal charter which guaranteed their community a large degree of autonomy.

At the beginning of the 13th century, Saint Quentin entered the royal domain. It developed a thriving textile and wine industry.

From the 14th century, Saint Quentin suffered from this strategic position: it endured the Hundred Years' War and in the 15th century, the city was disputed between the king of France and the dukes of Burgundy. Its population decreased from ten thousand to seven thousand due to the plague; subsequently, the economy suffered badly.

In the second half of the 17th century, the conquests of Louis XIV took Saint Quentin away from the border, and it lost much of its strategic role.

During the First French Empire, difficulties in the export market brought an economic decline. At the request of the municipality, Napoleon authorized the razing of the fortifications, to allow the city to grow beyond its old boundaries. In 1814-1815, Saint Quentin was occupied by the Russian army, but without significant damage.

In the 19th century, Saint Quentin developed into a thriving industrial city, thanks to entrepreneurs constantly on the lookout for new technologies. Textiles and mechanical products were foremost among a wide variety of products.

In 1870, during the Franco-Prussian War, the population repelled the invader on October 8, but the city fell during the second offensive.

Now it was 1918. The British and Australian forces were about to face a fierce attack by their enemy.

Robbie and Harry were trying to get some sleep in a trench that stunk of rotting corpses and human excrement. It was Harry who sensed something sinister was about to occur; it did.

The sound of artillery bellowed over the landscape, it was deafening. The first shells started to hit and they could see their comrades being blasted into the air. All they could do is crouch down in the trench and hope the next shell didn't have their name on it.

The devastation was incredible: how any of their troops could survive was a miracle.

Saint Quentin Cathedral Before Bombardment

After the Bombardment

Central Saint Quentin

The barrage of German shells caused massive destruction to the British, Australian and New Zealand lines with all communication lines cut. Once again pigeons were called upon to relay messages to the High Command.

The bombardment had persisted for an hour or two; Robbie and Harry were still alive!

Then a call went out: GAS!

They and all their comrades quickly donned their gas masks as the toxic mustard gas hit their trenches. This insidious gas permeated uniforms causing third degree burns. If the victim lived, they would have horrendous scarring for life.

Both soldiers survived that first attack but were reticent about their likely survival, given the intensity of the German shelling.

Five hours had passed when the bombardment ceased; Robbie and Harry knew what that meant.

The Germans unleashed their storm troopers; operating in small groups, they advanced quickly exploiting weak points in the decimated British defences.

These storm troopers would avoid heavily defended areas, leaving the infantry following behind to deal with them. The key was to isolate the British defences from each other, leaving them venerable to attack.

The storm troopers' tactic involved occupying enemy territory rapidly so as to disrupt communication by attacking enemy headquarters, artillery units and supply depots in the rear. Each division selected its best and fittest soldiers to man the storm units from which several new divisions were then formed. This process gave the German army an initial advantage in the attack but meant that the best troops would suffer disproportionately heavy casualties, while the quality of the men in reserve diminished..

The two friends fought gallantly using rifle and bayonet but the odds were stacked against them. Robbie was in a fierce struggle with a storm trooper; both were thrusting their bayonets trying to bring the other one down when Robbie was stabbed from behind. He slowly sank to his knees, then looked up to the heavens through glazed eyes. He received another bayonet thrust to his stomach by his original foe and he crumbled to the bottom of the trench. His body would never be found.
Harry fared better and although wounded by a rifle shot in the leg, would live to fight another day.

By the close of that fateful first day, the Germans had broken through the British first and second lines of defence along a quarter of the entire line attacked. Large parts of the Fifth Army were falling back. Static trench warfare had given way to mobile warfare for the first time since 1914. Southwest of Saint Quentin, the Ninth Irish Fusiliers' war diary reported that serious losses had been sustained.

In addition to losing the three battalions of the Forward Zone, the three battalions in the Battle Zone were reduced to two hundred and fifty men each and only the three reserve battalions were at reasonable strength. The fighting strength of the division now numbered less than three thousand men.

General Gough had been forced to order a fighting retreat to win time for reinforcements to reach his army. It was apparent, as the British fell back, that troops in the redoubts had been sacrificed to the German infantry. The right wing of the Third Army also retreated to avoid being outflanked. The morning fog had delayed the use of aircraft but, by the end of the day thirty six squadrons of the Royal Flying Corps had been in action and reported losing sixteen aircraft and crew, while having shot down fourteen enemy.

The first day of the battle had been very costly for the Germans. They suffered almost forty thousand casualties, slightly more than they inflicted on the British and Commonwealth forces. More seriously, the crucial attack in the north had failed to isolate the Flesquieres salient, which had been held by the renowned Sixty Third Division. The German attack was already beginning to head in the wrong direction, but that would have been of little comfort to General Gough and his men as darkness closed in on the first day of battle.

Where there is love there is life.
Mahatma Gandhi (1869-1948)

Chapter 11

Harry had been stretchered to the dressing station where his leg wound had been cleaned and bandaged.

Although not life threatening, the damage was quite substantial. The medical officer estimated it would be eight weeks before Harry would be fit enough to return to the front. Hospital beds were at a premium and were allocated to the badly wounded. The High Command devised a plan where soldiers and officers who required convalescing would be billeted to French homes and farms for the required period. The occupants of the house would be compensated. This actually worked out to be a cheaper alternative than hospital care.

Harry was billeted in a beautiful château near the village of Versailles with the Dampierre family. The patriarch of the family, Commandant Dampierre was serving in the French army, reporting to General Joffre.

Château de Dampierre

His wife, Madam Dampierre looked after the château and its three hundred acres of farmlands. Her son, Jacques, had been killed in the Battle of Mons at the age of nineteen. Her daughter had been sent away to Boston, America, to ensure her safety soon after Jacques died.

Harry had been allocated a small two-room apartment on the ground floor in consideration of his wound. It was not particularly luxurious, in fact it was in the servants' quarters but it was far superior to sleeping in the trenches at the front.

Every day one of the château's maids wheeled Harry around the estate. He loved the gardens and trees including century old oaks. After about an hour of walking they would come across a large lake. It was beautiful; water lilies floated on the edge and weeping willows were in abundance along its shores. A Japanese bridge crossed the lake at its narrowest point and this is where Harry and Marie would stop and contemplate. Harry could not speak much French and Marie knew no English so the conversations they had were fairly simplistic but they managed.

Marie's day off was Sunday; she always visited her family nearby. On these days Harry was left to his own devices. He usually read a book or simply sat in the wingback chair in his apartment and imagined what life would be like after this horrid war was over. He had decided he wouldn't be returning to Vauxhall. He had greater ambitions.

One Sunday, Madame Dampierre dropped by his quarters and asked Harry if he would like her to wheel him around the gardens. Harry was unsure. Madame Dampierre was far above his station in life.

'Monsieur Harry, I enjoy walking through the château's gardens and besides I am bored. Let me do this for you.'

'Thank you, Madame.'

'Would you like me to take you to the lake, Harry?

'Yes Madame, that is my favourite section of the garden.'

Madame Dampierre walked slowly and described how the gardens had evolved over the past two hundred years. She was very knowledgeable and knew the botanical names of the various plants and trees. After an hour or so they reached the lake. Harry requested they stop on the Japanese bridge.

'I love looking out over the lake from this bridge. It reminds me of a lake I used to visit back home in London.'

'Really? Where in London, Harry?'

'Hyde Park, Madame.'

'I have been to London several times but I have not visited Hyde Park. Next time my husband and I are there, I will make sure we visit.'

'I am sure you will enjoy it, Madame.'

'I better get you back, Harry. You must be feeling tired by now.

'Thank you.'

They returned by a different route and once again Madame Dampierre explained the design of the gardens and how they had evolved.

Harry enjoyed his afternoon and felt quite content when he returned to his small apartment.

Madame Dampierre returned to the château and reflected on how much she enjoyed the few hours she spent with the young Englishman.

Harry's convalescence was progressing well; although he hadn't attempted to walk, he felt his leg was healing and the sense of feeling was slowly returning.

The week progressed as normal. Marie took him for his daily excursion through the gardens and Harry continued to read various books lent to him by Madame Dampierre, including:

Anne's House of Dreams by L.M. Montgomery

His Last Bow by Arthur Conan Doyle

The Man with Two Left Feet by P.G. Wodehouse

In the Land of White Death by Valerian Albanov

A Short History of England by Mary Tyler

Harry had never been much of a reader but with all the spare time on his hands he soon discovered the wonderful world of literature and history.

Sunday arrived and Madame Dampierre once again offered Harry the opportunity to venture through the gardens. He was delighted as he enjoyed Madame's conversation as well as her extraordinary beauty. The fact that she was fluent in English made the afternoon that much more enjoyable.

'Harry, how long has it been since you were wounded?'

'Well, Madame let me see, it would have to be six weeks, yes six weeks. Why do you ask?'

'I was just thinking that it was time you tried to take a few steps.'

'I would like to but the army hasn't issued me with a pair of crutches yet. I was rather hoping I would have had them by now.'

'Well, why don't we try this? I'll stand a few steps away from you and see if you can raise yourself from the chair and walk to me.'

'Don't worry. I won't let you fall, I promise.'

Harry agreed and with all the strength in his arms pushed himself up and onto very shaky legs. He took his first step. Harry swayed back and forth for a little while and looking at Madame Dampierre directly in the eyes, made another step.

'Harry, you are doing beautifully. Just two more steps.'

Harry, with sheer determination, stumbled into the beautiful woman's arms.

'You made it, Harry! Well done.'

She was holding onto Harry to keep him upright, while he was holding onto her with lust in his heart. He could feel her breasts against him, the smell of her hair and perfume. It was intoxicating. She could feel his excitement and although tempted, knew it would be wrong to   seduce this young man. She was forty-four years old and Harry couldn't be much more than twenty, the same age as her beloved son.

Amelie Dampierre helped Harry to the wheelchair and they returned home to the château in an uneasy silence.

Amelie couldn't stop thinking about the young English soldier and their brief encounter in the gardens. She had not seen her husband, Commandant Dampierre, for six months and even then he had only three days at the château before he had to return again to the front. She was feeling lonely and a little amorous. She also knew she must not give in to her desires.

The following Sunday came and went without any contact with the Englishman. Harry was disappointed but had a pretty good idea why Madame Dampierre decided not to take him through the gardens. He too had not stopped thinking about her.

Madame Dampierre decided that she could not go another Sunday without seeing Harry. She walked down to his apartment only to find him walking in the small garden at the front of the building.

> 'Harry, you are walking!'

> 'Hello, Madame. Yes I have been exercising for a week now. I am determined to get well and return to the front and join my comrades in the fight.

> 'How far can you walk?'

> 'Unaided only a short distance but with the aid of a stick, I have been able to follow the path to the bridge and back.

> 'That's excellent! May I accompany you on the walk today?'

> 'I would be honoured, Madame.'

> 'Please call me Amelie.'

They walked albeit slowly along the path; their conversation was open and enjoyable. Harry only became quiet when she questioned him about the war and his experiences. He, like most soldiers, was reticent to talk about it to civilians.

The walk took much longer this time but Harry made it back without any discomfort. When they arrived at his apartment they sat on a bench seat in the pretty courtyard.

'Harry, would you care to join me for dinner in the château tonight? It won't be anything grand as the chef is on his day off?'

'Madame, I mean Amelie, are you sure? I wouldn't want to put you to any trouble just for me.'

'I would not have asked you if it was going to be a bother. Now I expect you at seven.'

'Thankyou, Amelie. I look forward to it.'

Harry polished his boots until you could see his face in them and pressed his uniform as best he could.

He hoped he wouldn't disgrace himself at the table; his parents had taught all their children proper table manners but nothing about the etiquette of eating in a château.

La Seduction

Chapter 12

The young soldier from East London walked up to the château's entrance and knocked on the large oak doors, doors that had adorned the château for over four hundred years. He made sure his shoes were still shining and his tie was centred and there was no lint on his uniform.

Amelie answered the door a few minutes later.

'Hello, Harry. You look wonderful. Come inside.'

Harry stepped in, not knowing what to expect and he was overwhelmed by the grandeur. The entrance room was magnificent with its beautiful gold leaf furniture and large portraits; these he assumed were members of the Dampierre family. An enormous crystal chandelier gave the room an ethereal glow. At the end of the grand room an ornate marble staircase rose to the upper levels; its red wood banisters and cast iron tulip panels ensured this was the château's centrepiece.

Amelie sensed Harry's bewilderment.

'Yes, I know it is a little ostentatious; the château has been in my husband's family for over six generations. Even if I wanted to redecorate I couldn't; it would be seen as sacreligious.

'Follow me into the salon, we can have a wine before dinner is served.'

Harry waited for Amelie to indicate where he should sit. She sat down on a chaise longue and beckoned him to join her.

'Could please open the bottle of champagne Harry?'

'Yes of course Madame; I mean Amelie.'

Harry opened the bottle of 1901 vintage Dom Pérignon. He had no idea this was premium champagne as he had never tasted anything other than cheap wine and beer. He poured the wine into the crystal flutes but did not realise he needed to pour it slowly. The expensive champagne spilled out of the flutes and onto the antique coffee table. Amelie laughed.

'Cheri, let me show you the correct way to pour champagne.'

She showed the embarrassed young soldier how champagne should be served without making him feel ill at ease.

They made their way into the intimate dining room and took their places at the table. One of the château's senior butlers served the dinner.

'Amelie, I thought you said all the servants were on their days off.'

'Jean will be leaving us when we have completed our meal, Harry, you have no need to worry.

'I am not worried, just a little embarrassed; I have never been served by a butler before.

'You're my guest, Harry, you should just relax and enjoy. Do you like my coq au vin?'

'I do. So, you cooked this yourself, Amelie?'

'Of course. I said I would.'

'Sorry.'

'No need to apologise.'

'How do you like the wine I chose, Harry?'

It was the most beautiful wine he had ever tasted not that he had had the opportunity of tasting many wines.

'It is very nice.'

'Good. I took it from my husband's wine cellar; he only keeps the best wines.'

The wine was a 1900 Chateau Lafitte regarded as one of the best wines produced in Bordeaux.'

After they had finished the meal, they moved back to the salon.

'Would you like a glass of cognac?'

Harry had heard of cognac but certainly had never tasted it.

'Yes, I would love one,' he said confidently.

He was starting to get the hang of living the high life.

Amelie took the bottle of 100-Year Old Louis XIII Cognac from the liquor cabinet and two large brandy balloons.

'I don't know about you, Harry, but I prefer to warm the glass in my hands for ten minutes or so rather than use the brandy warmer.'

'I agree. Much better than the brandy warmer,' Harry said, without having any idea what he was talking about. He would just follow Amelie's lead.

He sipped the century-old cognac, following Amelie's lead once again; he had never tasted anything so magnificent, so smooth, so wonderful.

'I don't believe this; here I am sipping 100 year old cognac with a beautiful aristocratic woman in a centuries old chateau and in a few weeks I will be back in the trenches crawling over bomb-cratered fields and trying not to get killed. I'll be eating beef jerky out of a can and drinking lukewarm tea certainly not coq au vin, fine red wine and cognac. I am sorry, Amelie but I am way out of my depth. I'm just a humble soldier from East London who happened to get a couple of bullets in his leg and was lucky enough to be billeted here. I really think I should go.'

'Mon Chéri you are a beautiful young man, a brave man, a warrior and you are more than worthy of dining in my home.'

Amelie rose from the lounge took Harry's hand and led him out of the room.

Harry was dumbfounded. He was being led like a little puppy, so he just followed obediently. After ascending the staircase, Amelie led him to her boudoir.

'Mon Chéri, I want you to spend the night with me.'

They entered the elegant room with a gilt-edged four-poster bed, the centrepiece of the room.

She did not speak; she simply undressed him, never taking her eyes off his. He was trying not to show his nervousness while at the same time, his excitement was building.

Amelie stepped back and admired the young man's physique.

'You are a beautiful man, Harry.'

She slowly undressed and again, her eyes did not leave his; when she was naked she approached Harry gently, kissed his lips and led him to the bed.

He had only been with a whore at "Maison de Plaisir" and that was only a few times when he had been on leave. He was hardly experienced. He needn't have worried. Amelie was an excellent teacher. They made love for what seemed like hours.

Harry woke when the sun started to shine through the drapes. Looking over at Amelie, he saw she looked so angelic yet so erotic, with a breast exposed and her long blonde hair cascading over her shoulders. He leaned over and kissed her cheek. Her eyes opened and she pulled Harry to her. They made love again before Harry slipped out via the tradesman's entrance, hoping not to be seen by any staff.

Harry and Amelie had an intimate relationship for the next two weeks until Harry was called back to the front. Within two days of departing from the château, Harry was fighting Germans, eating beef jerky out of the can and dodging bullets. He had wonderful memories and for that he was thankful.

Soon after Harry departed, Commandant Dampierre returned home on leave. He always enjoyed coming home and seeing his beautiful Amelie.

On his arrival, Jean, the senior butler, asked if he could speak with his master.

'Sir, I am sorry but I have some disturbing news.'

Jean described what had been going on between the English soldier and his mistress.

Maurice Dampierre was furious and stormed inside, calling for his wife. Amelie appeared, wondering what was going on. When her husband normally arrived home on leave, they would make love; now he was shouting at her.

'Amelie, have you been having an affair with that little English upstart while I have been fighting a war?'

'Of course not! Who told you such lies?'

'Jean maintains he saw this man leave in the mornings early, having arrived in the evenings. That can only mean one thing. Madame, you are an adulteress and a whore!'

Dampierre pulled his sword from its scarab and thrust it into Amelie's heart, pinning her against the wall. He left her there.

Dampierre ran to his car and ordered his driver to get him back to the front at once.

Commandant Maurice Dampierre was killed in action the following day.

Harry never learned about the death of his lover.

Racing Birds

Chapter 13

Percy Shaw was a very proud man, his family had lived in Sheffield in Yorkshire for many decades and he was the fifth generation to work in the coalmines at Elsecar Colliery. The work was hard and dirty; he returned home from the mines and scrubbed himself in the laundry basin located in the little outbuilding in the backyard of the tenement house they leased from the mining company. He would then go into the house, kiss his wife, Emily, and disappear out the back to tend to his beloved pigeons until six o'clock when his dinner was served in the kitchen.

Percy and Emily had four children, two girls and two boys with the youngest being Elizabeth, aged ten. The next was Tim, aged twelve, Katherine, fourteen and the eldest, Joe, aged seventeen.

Joe shared his father's love for racing pigeons and had twelve of his own. Percy kept over sixty in a loft he and Joe constructed from wood they had collected around the mine site. Joe had recently joined his father working at the mine and although it was hard work, he enjoyed the comradeship and the pay cheque at the end of the working week.

Percy was fiercely competitive. He had won more short course races than anybody else in the district. His main rival was the local green grocer, Fred Laughton. Fred had over one hundred birds and was only one shy of equalling Percy's record. Fred's eldest son,

Fred Laughton in Front of His Shop

Don went to school with Joe. They were good mates, although the same could not be said for Percy and Fred.

Racing day was Sunday, the one day they all had off. The pigeon owners would drive sixty miles in their automobiles to a designated spot where they would release their pigeons. Each bird had a leg ring with a specific code. When the birds arrived back at the coop, the ring would be inserted into a racing clock and the time would be recorded. The fastest racing pigeons have been clocked at over one hundred miles per hour.

This was truly the working man's sport, frowned on by the middle classes but adopted in its long course format by the aristocracy, including Royalty.

Red Dove owned and raced by Mr Fred Laughton won this race; Fred had equalled Percy's record and now the competition was on. Fred and Percy detested each other so the competition was fierce.

August 1915 Yorkshire

The war had been going for a full year with some success for Britain and its Commonwealth Allies. The Western Front had evolved into a line of trenches stretching from Belgium to the Swiss border. Communication between the battlefield and HQ was essential; the radio, although effective, was continually destroyed by enemy shelling. The most effective long haul communication was pigeons. Pigeons played a vital part in World War One as they proved to be an extremely reliable way of sending messages. Such was the importance of pigeons that over one hundred thousand were used in the war with an astonishing success rate, ninety five per cent getting through to their destination with their message.

The British Government needed all the birds they could get and, like the horses they requisitioned, they also requisitioned pigeons from their devoted owners.

War Birds

Chapter 14

September 1915 Yorkshire

It was a cold and windy day when the army officer knocked on the door of number 10 Cromwell Street, Sheffield. Emily Shaw opened the door.

The Shaw Residence

'Yes, how can I help you?'

'Is your husband home, Mrs? I need to discuss a very important matter in relation to the war effort.'

'Goodness me, he's over fifty! You can't take him.'

'Don't worry, we don't want to take him. It's his birds we want to take.'

'Oh, he won't part with his pigeons. They're his pride and joy. He cares more about his birds than he does about me or the kids.'

Just then Percy arrived home from another hard day at the mines. Joe was with him.

'What's going on here then?' asked Percy.

'Hello Sir, my name is Captain Perry, I would like a few moments of your time if I could.'

'Alright Captain but I need to clean up first. Mrs Shaw will show you into the kitchen; you never know, she may even make you a nice cup of tea.'

'Come on, Joe, we better clean ourselves up for the Captain.'

Percy and his son disappeared out back to the laundry to scrub the black soot from their faces and hair as well as their filthy hands.

'Why do you think that army captain is here, Pop?'

'Well, Joe, it's not to recruit me. I'm too bloody old and you're too bloody young, so I don't know.'

Once cleaned, they went into the kitchen and joined Emily and the Captain. A cup of tea had just been poured.

'So, Captain Perry what do we owe the honour?'

'Well, as you know the war has being going on for about a year and much to our disappointment it doesn't look like ending any time soon. One of the key issues in fighting this war is communications and we have discovered one of the most effective methods of communication is the employment of homing pigeons. Therefore it is my job to find and acquire sufficient number of pigeons to meet our requirements.'

'Hold on Captain, there are no birds here for sale. These pigeons are my life and I will not sell a single one.'

Feeding Pigeons

'Mr Shaw, I am afraid you don't have a say in the matter; if I choose your birds, I am empowered by the war act to acquire them, at a fair price of course.'

'So, you bastards can just come here and take my beautiful birds and I can't do a bloody thing about it? Well it stinks!'

'Think of it as your contribution to the war effort, Mr Shaw.'

'The war effort, be buggered! When do you intend to take them?'

'Now, I am afraid; the transport is parked in the street.'

'I don't even have time to spend with them before they go,' Percy said with teary eyes.

'We will leave you with three cocks and three hens which will enable you to build up your stocks again.'

'Yeah, that would be right! Once I build up again, you will be back to take them again.'

'How much are you going to pay me?'

'The Government has authorised me to pay you one pound per bird.'

'What! One pound! Some of my best are worth ten pounds and the rest would bring five.'

'I am sorry, Mr Shaw, but that is the amount the army can offer you. I suggest you decide which birds you are keeping, as we need to load the others up and move on. We have one more call to make before darkness hits.'

'I think darkness has already hit. From whom else are you stealing?'

'Careful, Mr Shaw. We are visiting Mr Laughton as he has over one hundred pigeons.'

'So, there is some justice in this world.'

Captain Perry accompanied Percy out to his coop and waited for him to select the six birds he would keep. Among them was "Red", his champion.

Two soldiers arrived with portable cages and started loading them. Once filled, they took them out to a Double Decker bus which would be their home on the fields of France and Belgium.

London Bus Pigeon Coop

Young Joe asked Captain Perry who would be caring for the pigeons when they were on the front. The Captain informed him that soldiers who showed some interest in the birds were appointed.

He decided then and there that he would lie about his age and join the army to assure him and his father that their pigeons were being well looked after.

He approached his father with the idea.

'Pop, I have a great idea. Why don't I enlist? With my experience racing pigeons, they would surely appoint me as a handler.'

'Son you are only seventeen; the required age is eighteen.'

'Harry down the road enlisted and he was only sixteen. You just lie about your age and if you sign the form, everything will be all right.

'Let me talk to your mother and I'll let you know in the morning.'

Percy and Emily spoke about it that night and although Emily was reluctant at first, Percy convinced her that the pigeon buses were well away from the firing line and their son would be relatively safe, safer than being in the trenches. She agreed.

The next day young Joe enlisted at the town hall and was given, and subsequently passed, the physical. He was issued with his uniform and the remainder of his kit.

While enlisting, he told the enlistment officer of his experience with birds etc. He was sent away to basic training and six weeks later, arrived in Egypt. After a few weeks of training in horrendous heat and visiting the pyramids and other tourist sites, he was dispatched to France along with the 31st Division. On arrival, they were transported to the Somme. He fought and died on the first day of "The Battle of the Somme", along with twenty thousand other British soldiers. He was an ordinary foot soldier; unbeknown to him, his beloved pigeons were instrumental in communicating dispatches along the front.

One of the handlers of these magnificent pigeons was Fred Laughton.

Don't Shoot the Messenger

Chapter 15

Fred Laughton had no idea his good pal, Joe Shaw, had been killed on the infamous first day of the Battle of the Somme. He had assumed that he too was a pigeon handler somewhere else on the Western Front.

Fred felt relatively safe as the red Double Decker Bus where his pigeons were housed had to be close to the High Command so messages could be taken and attached to the birds for dispatch to the front. That's not to say that he didn't feel nervous with the noise of shellfire and machine gunfire constantly in the background.

He figured that if the Generals were close, he was safe; they didn't place themselves in dangerous situations.

The fighting troops were in a different situation. They were either holed up in trenches or were attacking over no man's land. In the situations where they were able to break through the German lines, the messenger pigeons played a critical role. Their messages would direct artillery fire and divulge enemy troop movements.

Harry Andersen was a private in the 1st London Brigade, a Royal Fusilier; his life couldn't be more different from his job as a fitter and turner at Vauxhall in East London.

There were about fifty fusiliers holed up in an abandoned barn, fighting off an intensive German attack well behind enemy lines. They were running out of ammunition and knew they needed help. The Officer leading the unit, Captain

McKinney, decided to use one of the three pigeons remaining to dispatch a message to HQ, giving them their position and the location of the attacking troops. He requested artillery to shell the Krauts and give them relief.

Harry was responsible for the birds; he folded the message and attached it to the message cylinder attached to the bird's leg. He threw the pigeon up and Tommy flew off.

It reached about five hundred feet when a German rifleman shot it down.

Harry took the next bird and completed the same procedure. It too reached five hundred feet and was shot out of the sky.

The last pigeon was Harry's favourite, Prefect; he carefully took it out of the basket, attached the message and wished his mate 'bon voyage'. Prefect rose into the smoke- filled sky. Harry thought he had made it, but, alas, Prefect dropped to the ground with a bullet through his wing. Harry and the rest of the Platoon were devastated as that was their last chance. Then, amazingly, Prefect started to flap his wings and eventually rose into the battlefield sky, avoiding extensive enemy fire. Thirty minutes later, a bombardment began knocking out the German attack. Prefect had made it!

When the platoon returned back to their line, they inquired about the fate of the heroic bird. He had been treated by the medics and, in their opinion, should be fine to fly another day.

Prefect had saved fifty Royal Fusiliers.

Happy Birthday, General
Chapter 16

The British General was looking forward to his birthday bash. It was to celebrate his fiftieth and, although he would have preferred to be at home in Cambridge with his wife and family, he nonetheless hoped it would be a memorable one. The date was 21st March, 1918.

The château was the perfect venue to hold such a function with its ornate dining rooms and reception halls plus a kitchen that could prepare meals for one hundred diners.

The dinner would be catering for twenty so, the venue would be more than satisfactory.

The chef had suggested a menu that would be simple, yet delicious.

> *Chicken Liver Pâté*
> *Bread*
> *Selection of Cheeses*
> *Coquilles St-Jacques (Gratinéed Scallops)*
> *Winter Salad with Buttermilk Dressing*
> *Blanquette de Veau (Veal in Cream Sauce)*
> *Surprise Dessert*

The dinner was due to begin at seven o'clock with aperitifs at six pm.

The General's second in command, Lieutenant Colonel Smithton, had planned the event. He was confident that the evening would go off without a hitch.

The officers started arriving about six and were offered champagne from the General's private cellar on arrival.

'I say, this champagne is rather nice don't you think Bradshaw?'

'Certainly is Worthington, do you know what it is?'

'No, but I'll check the bottle when the orderly comes around again.'

'Oh, here we are, he's back already, can I look at the bottle, corporal? Ah I should have known, Dom Pérignon.'

'Bloody nice drop. Must organise my man to order some in.'

'General Bradshaw, how do you think the war's going for us?'

'Well, I think that with the Americans joining the fray at last, we have got the Hun on the back foot.'

'Yes, I agree with you, General, although we haven't seen too many doughboys yet. I am told it won't be long before we have a million of the buggers over here fighting shoulder to shoulder with our boys.'

The dinner bell rang and they moved into the dining room where they were seated by the orderlies in their correct places determined by an agreed seating plan.

The wine had been selected by General Haigen and was regarded as a selection of the finest French wines available.

The majority of the wines came from his favourite winemaker, Domaine De La Romanee-Conti.

His selection included:

La Tache Pinot Noir.

Montrachet Chardonnay

Romanee-Conti burgundy

Chateau d'Yquem Dessert Wine

Brigadier Watson said grace and then the entrée was served. There was plenty of conversation and laughter amongst the officers as well as serious discussion about the war and the likely outcome.

At nine o'clock the great doors were opened and four junior offices entered, carrying a very large fruit platter. What was special about this particular platter was the fact that a beautiful young woman, completely naked, was reclining amongst the exotic fruits. Fruit was also positioned on strategic parts of her body. The officers applauded and began to enjoy the dessert with particular interest in the fruit adorning the body.

The doors opened once more and music permeated throughout the dining room. Twenty young women, all nearly naked, attracted the officers' attention gliding like angels around the long table. One by one, they sat on the lap of an officer until they were all paired.

The next sixty minutes was like a Roman Orgy until a Major arrived and insisted on seeing General Haigen. General Haigen kept the Major waiting for forty-five minutes but managed to drag himself away from the dinner.

'What is it Major? I am celebrating my birthday and I don't wish to keep my guests waiting.'

'I am sorry, Sir, but this is urgent.'

'Well, what is it man?'

'Sir, the Germans have launched a major offensive.'

'Good God, where?'

'Saint Quentin.'

While the Generals and senior officers were cavorting, the men for whom they were responsible were being slaughtered.

The artillery bombardment began at four forty am with an intensive German barrage opening on British positions south west of Saint Quentin for a depth of two to four miles. A heavy German barrage opened up simultaneously along the whole forty-mile front. Trench mortars, mustard gas, chlorine gas, tear gas and smoke canisters were concentrated on the forward trenches, while heavy artillery bombarded rear areas to destroy Allied artillery and supply lines. Troops, horses, transport and guns suffered heavily. Over three and a half million shells were fired in five hours hitting targets over an area of one hundred and fifty square miles; this was the biggest barrage of the entire war. It hit all areas of the British front occupied by Fifth Army, most of the front of Third Army, and some of the front of the First Army to the north. In total, the British suffered seven thousand five hundred casualties during this bombardment alone. The front line was badly damaged and communications were cut with the rear zone, which was severely disrupted. To the British command this was an unpleasant surprise, certainly not what General Haigen had expected for his birthday.

When the infantry assault began between six am and nine forty, the storm trooper tactics were a stunning success. Dawn broke to reveal a heavy morning mist. By five am, visibility was barely ten yards in places, and the fog was extremely slow to dissipate throughout the morning. The fog (combined with smoke from the bombardments of both sets of artillery) made visibility poor throughout the day allowing the storm troopers to penetrate deep into the British positions undetected. Most forward positions were overwhelmed and nearly all of the British front line fell during the morning. British communications were soon in a shambles; telephone wires had been cut by artillery and runners had a difficult time finding their way through the dense fog and heavy shelling. There was chaos, as forward positions could not communicate with Battalion and Divisional Headquarters or the artillery.

Happy Birthday, General Haigen!

Red Cross Heroine

Edith Cavell

Chapter 17

The Reverend Frederick Cavell and his young wife Louisa had been assigned by the church to the little town of Swardeston in Norfolk. This was the reverend's first assignment since he had been ordained just three months before in August 1863.

Swardeston is a village four miles south of Norwich in Norfolk, England, on high ground above the Tas valley.

One of the earliest mentions of Swardeston is in the Domesday Book where it is mentioned amongst the lands given to Roger Bigod by King William. The manor given to Bigod included 45 acres of land and 2 acres of meadow.

Its church, dedicated to St Mary the Virgin, has a 15th century tower, but two arched windows indicate that its origins are Saxon and Norman.

Swardeston Anglican Church

On December the fourth, 1865, Louisa had their first child whom they named Edith Louisa. Edith would become a household name in both Britain and Belgium.

Edith was the eldest of four children; Florence, Lilian and John were born with only a one-year gap between each of them. The children were home- schooled in the vicarage and all proved to be quick learning.

In 1884, Edith, now sixteen, was sent off to boarding school in Kessington followed by Clevedon near Bristol. Her final school was Laurel Court in Peterborough. Edith excelled in her studies particularly in French for which she had a real talent.

On leaving school, she became a governess and was much loved by the children in her charge.

Edith travelled to Austria and Bavaria in 1888 and was most impressed with the free hospital run by Dr Wolfberg. This experience kindled her interest in nursing.

In 1890, Edith became a governess to a family in Brussels and returned home to Swardeston for her summer breaks.

In 1895, her father became seriously ill and she returned home to nurse him. This experience was cathartic and she decided to make nursing her chosen career.

Edith Cavell

Edith was accepted for nurse training at the Royal London Hospital under Eva Luckes.

A typhoid epidemic broke out in Maidstone, Kent. With the help of five other nurses only one hundred and thirty two people died out of the seventeen hundred who contracted the disease. Edith received the "Maidstone Medal" for her work. She had built a very good reputation in nursing and in 1907 she returned to Brussels at the invitation of D Antoine Depage. Soon after he opened his pioneering "L'École Belge d'Infirmières Diplômées", he asked Edith to run it. By 1912, Edith's training program had produced many well-qualified nurses who were in much demand.

The First World War erupted in July 1914. Edith decided to stay in Belgium and continue her work.

On the 20th of August, German soldiers invaded and occupied Brussels where fierce fighting took place and the wounded from all participating nations started to pour into Edith's clinic. The clinic was declared a Red Cross hospital; all staff was instructed not to show any allegiance to one side over the other.

As the war progressed and battles such as The Battle of Mons raged, British soldiers who were heavily outnumbered, retreated. In the confusion, many soldiers were cut off behind German lines. The Germans hunted them down, summarily shooting them and the villagers who sheltered them.

1915

Edith hid two British soldiers at the clinic and helped them escape. She was approached by an underground organisation to join them and help other trapped soldiers to escape to neutral territory; despite the danger, she agreed.

Over the next several months, Edith hid almost two hundred allied soldiers at the Berkendael Institute while they were waiting to be ferried across the border.

On July 31st 1915, Phillipe Baucq and another member of the escape team were arrested. The Germans discovered letters incriminating Edith Cavell and on August 5th the secret police arrested her.

Edith was questioned for seventy-two hours and was forced to make a confession.

She was detained in solitary confinement until the beginning of her trial, which began on October 7th.

There were over thirty other defendants from the underground on trial.

Edith confessed to helping allied soldiers escape, and,found guilty of treason, she was sentenced to death. America and Spain made strong diplomatic efforts to have her sentence reduced but to no avail.

The English chaplain, Stirling Gahan found Edith calm when he visited her to give the sacrament. She assured him she was not afraid

'*Standing as I do in view of God and Eternity, I realise that patriotism is not enough, I must have no hatred or bitterness towards anyone.* '

October 12th - At 2am Edith Cavell, Philippe Baucq and the three other Belgian men were taken to the Tir National shooting range in Schaerbeek, where they were executed.

Edith was buried in a grave marked by a wooden cross next to St. Gilles Prison.

1918, October 12th - On the third anniversary of her death, Queen Alexandra on the grounds of Norwich Cathedral, unveiled a memorial for Edith Cavell near a home for nurses, which also bears her name.

November 11th - World War One ended.

May 1919. Edith's body was exhumed from the Tir National in Brussels and a memorial service was held. The King and Queen of Belgium attended. Her body was then returned to England.

May 19th - Edith's body was taken from Dover to Victoria Station. It was then carried with great ceremony to Westminster Abbey for a memorial service attended by many VIPs including Queen Adelaide.

May 19th - During the afternoon, Edith's body was taken by special train from Liverpool Street to Thorpe Station, Norwich for a burial service at Norwich Cathedral led by Bishop Pollock. She was reburied just outside the east end of Norwich Cathedral in an area called "Life's Green".

Thank God I'm a Country Boy
Chapter 18

Dick Bailey was a country boy having been brought up on a farm in East Gippsland in Victoria, Australia. His family owned a substantial acreage near Bairnsdale where they grew wool and milked two hundred dairy cattle.

Dick and his five brothers and sisters helped around the farm. Dick, being the eldest, knew that one day he would inherit the entire estate.

In 1914, Dick was aged seventeen and was well aware that lads from the area were enlisting into the Australian Army to go half way across the world to fight for their King and country. He approached his parents to receive their blessing and sign their names on the enlistment form, which would elevate his age to eighteen.

'Dad, Mum, I have something very important to discuss with you.'

'I think I might know what that might be, Dick. The answer is no!'

'You don't even know what I want to talk to you about.'

'Really, well let me guess. 'I have decided to enlist in the army and go off to war.' Am I right?'

'Well, I guess you are, but I don't understand why you are both so much against it.'

'Son, you are seventeen, you have a wonderful future ahead of you. We both love you very much and we don't want to lose you.'

'But, Dad, this is an opportunity of a lifetime. I promise you I won't get killed. You know me... you're always telling me I'm the lucky one.'

'Let us sleep on it, Dick, and we'll talk about it again in the morning.'

The two concerned parents discussed the situation when they went to bed that night; they concluded that Dick would find a way regardless to join the fray and therefore they were better off agreeing and signing the papers. They conveyed their decision to their eldest son the next morning.

Dick was delighted and raced off to the adjoining farm where his best mate Dan lived.

'Hey, Dan. Guess what! I'm joining up.'

'You can't, you're not old enough, you silly bugger.'

'Mum and Dad have agreed to sign the papers.'

'Well, I'll be fucked, you lucky bastard. Maybe my folks will agree to sign mine too.'

'Yeah, that's what I was hoping for,so we could both go marching off to war together; best mates, brothers in arms.'

'When do you leave, mate?'

'Fucked if I know, I haven't even been into Bairnsdale to enlist yet. I'll probably ride in tomorrow. Dad needs some stuff at Smith's Hardware so I can kill two birds with one stone.'

'Jesus, mate, you're so lucky.'

'Well, Dan, you better get off your skinny arse and put the white heat on your folks.'

'Gunna, tonight after dinner, they're always a bit mellow after a good feed.'

The following morning Dick was saddling up his horse and cart for the trip into town when he saw Dan riding like the proverbial wind across the paddocks.

'Don't fucking leave without me, ya bastard.'

'They agreed? I don't believe it. Well done, Dan!'

'Yep, when they heard you were going, they knew they couldn't say no.'

'This is fucking great! Beauty.'

The two young East Gippslanders rode into Bairnsdale, the first stage of their journey of adventure.

Both enlisted and passed the physical and they were told to report back the following Monday where they would board the troop train along with the other one hundred and fifty new recruits from the area and head for the Broadmeadows training camp.

The Army training camp became an excellent training program for where they would end up in Flanders which was a muddy slippery hellhole. Many of the soldiers contracted diseases including dysentery. After six weeks of living and training in these horrid conditions, they received word they were shipping out.

The first step in their long and arduous journey was a ship to Albany, Western Australia. The boys camped there for ten days before boarding a large troop ship, "The Star of Victoria", heading for Egypt.

January 1915

The journey took six weeks and the weather was magnificent with sunny days and smooth seas, for about seven days. Throughout the remainder of the voyage, the young recruits endured rough seas, constant rain squalls and seasickness.

They did get some relief playing "two up", reading and keeping a diary.

At last the "Spirit of Victoria" berthed in Alexandria, Egypt.

The troops disembarked and created a tent city in the desert sands; it was not to be for long as they transferred to Mena camp on the outskirts of Cairo ten days later.

Mena Camp Egypt

The two now worldly Australians decided that they would be known as Daniel and Richard,names much more befitting soldiers of the AIF.

At the first opportunity, they walked the ten minutes to the pyramids and climbed the Great Pyramid. They both felt euphoric; this was an experience they would never have dreamed of back in East Gippsland.

His parents had given Daniel a camera and he took a photo of the camp from the top of the Great Pyramid.

Camp Taken from the Pyramids.

Y.M.C.A building

Brigade Headquarters.

Office OC Coy.

Back at Mena they settled into their tent, one of hundreds that made up the Australian Camp.

They were forced to march in the searing heat with full packs; this was to get them used to what it would be like when they were sent to war.

A few weeks passed and after several trips into Cairo and experiencing its temptations, they were itching to enter the fray.

The orders came down that they were to board a troop ship taking them to Turkey. Most of the Diggers had never heard of Turkey, other than as a fucking big bird you ate at Christmas.

The time came and the Anzacs were loaded onto the troopship. It wasn't going to be a cruise; they were squeezed like sardines.

A few days later they dropped anchor off Suvla Bay, where they waited in the darkness until they were lowered into the landing boats at about three am, then they were towed to the shore. A hail of bullets and shellfire greeted their landing.

Both Diggers survived the horrendous conditions and fierce fighting for the duration. They were evacuated along with the other Anzac and British troops to fight another day, this time in France and Belgium.

Retreat From Gallipoli

V.C. or V.D.

Chapter 19

Daniel and Richard spent another month in Egypt before being shipped off to The Western Front to face the German foe.

They were given four days' leave before being assigned to the Western Front.

They decided, as most of their Battalion did, to spend their time in Poperinge.

'What are we going to do in Pops, mate? I hear it's a pretty wild sort of a town. They say if ya can't get it in Pops, you're never gunna get it.

'Yeah, so I hear, mate. I think we should wait till we get there tomorrow. Get the lay of the land, as it were!'

The boys arrived about lunchtime and were astounded how many troops there were walking the streets and eating in the many eating-places. They managed to get a table in a small, out of the way café.

'Well mate, I have decided what I'm gunna do tonight,' Richard said with some conviction.

'Have you? What?'

'One of the other Diggers told me about this place called "Maison de Plaisir."

'What you mean? A fucking brothel?'

'Yeah, with the emphasis on fucking, I had my first in Bairnsdale earlier this year with this sheila I met. Fantastic… can't wait to have another.'

'Well, Richard, or should I go back to calling you Dick, count me out.'

'Suit yourself, my little virgin soldier mate.'

'How do you know if I'm a virgin or not?'

'Are You?'

'Bloody hell, yeah I am, but I don't plan paying some French whore to be my first.

'Please yourself; I'll meet you back at the billet later on.'

'What are you gunna do with yourself?'

'Dunno, I might wander over to Talbot house and see who's there, play some cards, have a chat with a few of the lads… I'll see.'

'Fair enough, see ya a little later on when I've lost some weight.'

'Yeah, whatever.'

Richard sauntered off down the paved streets looking for the infamous Maison de Plaisir; it didn't take him long: the red light was a dead give away, as was the sight of groups of soldiers standing outside in the street.

Richard went directly to the red painted door and knocked three times. A buxom middle-aged woman, heavily painted, opened the door and beckoned him in.

'Bonsoir, my name is Madame Fifi. How can I help you?'

'Madame, I would like your finest young lady.'

'Would you now,? Well, if you have five francs you can have Cloe.'

'If that is your recommendation, Madame, I will take her.'

Richard paid his five francs and Madame Fifi escorted him into the waiting area, the staircase up to the fourth floor. She informed him of the room number on the first floor. He fell in line with the other amorous soldiers, each waiting his turn.

One hour had passed when another buxom woman, younger than Fifi, beckoned him. He followed her into a private alcove; she smiled and got down on her knees where she proceeded to play the piccolo expertly. Just when he thought he was about to explode, she returned his instrument to its case and led him into Cloe's room.

Cloe was beautiful, everything he had hoped for and more. She took his hand, leading him to the large bed and undressed him slowly. One hour later he floated out of the room and onto the busy Pops street. He wandered back to his billet house where he found Daniel fast asleep, snoring.

In the morning they swapped stories, with Daniel feeling envious in one way and relieved in another.

'How was it, Richard?'

'Fucking great, mate, I thought the sheila back home was good but nothing like Cloe. As they say, no amateur ever won a world title.'

'Well, I hope you didn't pick up a dose of the clap.'

'No way, mate she was as clean as a whistle.'

'I hope you're right.'

At the end of their leave they were ordered to report to the British base headquarters in Ypres. They undertook additional training in shooting and bayonet practice as well as lectures on trench warfare and tactics.

Daniel was lying on his stretcher reading a book, *The Mysterious Stranger*, by Mark Twain. Richard entered the tent looking very dejected.

'What's up, mate? You look like your dog just died.'

'I think I've got the clap.'

'Why? What makes you think so?'

'It hurts when I piss and there's gunk coming out of my dick.'

'Have you been to the medical tent to get it checked out?'

'Nope, I'm too shit scared to find out.'

'Don't be bloody ridiculous! You've got to get it treated or you'll be in deep trouble. You can die from syphilis.'

'Yeah, I suppose you're right. I can't fucking believe I got the clap.'

'I'm not gunna tell ya I told you so.'

'Good. I'd hit you if you did.'

'Do you want me to walk with you over to the medical tent?'

'Na, I'll be right, I'll catch up with you a bit later.'

'Good luck, mate.'

'Thanks, I think I'm gunnna need it.'

Richard walked gingerly to the Medical Tent. He thought about turning around and going back but common sense got the better of him.

He entered the tent and was confronted with many soldiers wounded and nurses and doctors attending the poor blighters.

A nurse approached him asking what medical problem he had.

'I think I've got the clap, nurse,' he said with embarrassment.

'I see. Well, sit over there on that bench. Someone will get to you when we have time away from treating the wounded. That's our real priority.'

Richard sat there for two hours observing soldiers with war wounds being brought in and taken out. He felt ashamed that he was there to be treated for the clap and these boys were heroes, warriors. He hadn't seen even a German helmet, let alone the enemy.

Finally a nurse appeared and instructed him to follow her into a canvas cubicle.

'Well, soldier, I believe you have got yourself into some trouble?'

'Yes, nurse, I'm afraid so.'

'What are your symptoms?'

'I have started to get pain when I urinate.'

'Anything else?'

'I have gunk oozing out of my penis.'

'How long ago did you have sex?'

'Four days ago, when I was on leave in Poperinge.'

'All right, take your trousers and underpants off. Come on, quick smart. I bet you weren't embarrassed in front of the whore that gave you this condition.'

'No, nurse, I guess I wasn't, but it's different with you, you're'

'OK, let's have a look at you. It doesn't look too bad but you're going to need treatment which will take you out of your battalion for a couple of weeks.'

'I see. Well I just hope I don't miss out on some real action.'

'You've had all the action you need for the moment, soldier.'

Richard endured urethral syringes twice a day and was forced to drink copious amounts of milk. His was not a happy time.

Fromelles 19th July 1916

Daniel's battalion, the 59^{th,} had been ordered to march to the small town of Fromelles. There, they were instructed to begin digging their defensive trenches. This turned out to be a difficult task as the water table was very close to the surface so the troops were constantly digging in mud. The Anzacs had to pile sand bags as high as they could without being a hindrance to them going "over the top" when they were ordered to attack.

The Germans had been entrenched in their bunker system for two years; they observed every move the Australians were making. Once the trenches were finally dug, it became a waiting game.

On the 16th of July 1916 the officers informed the troops the bombardment was due to begin and would last three days, to blast the Germans out of their trenches. The worst day in Australia's wartime history was about to begin.

19 July 1916

Daniel was in the trench with his cobbers from the 59th; they had been listening to the bombardment of the German positions for hours now.

'Geez I hope the officers were right; this bombardment should knock the shit out of Fritz. Just a quick sprint and we take the German trenches.'

'You're bloody mad, Daniel, it's not gunna be that easy,' said Frankie, 'no bloody way.'

'I was only joking, Frankie; are you a bit scared mate?'

'Fucking oath mate, I really don't want to die here, I was rather hoping I would die on the job with my Mrs.'

'Yeah, me too,' said Daniel.

The officers started to move along the trenches, informing the Diggers that they were due to go over the top in thirty minutes. They stressed to the troops to check their equipment, most importantly their rifles, bayonets and grenades.

Daniel took the time to write a quick note to his Mum and Dad, back home in East Gippsland.

"Dear Mum and Dad,

I have been told we are going over the top very soon. I know what that is like from my time at Gallipoli so I'm not really looking forward to it. I made it out of Gallipoli so I have no doubt I will survive here with the help of God.

I will put this letter in my pocket and if anything does happen to me, my cobbers will find it and send it on to you.

I want you to know that I love you both..

Well I said a quick note and there's the five-minute whistle so I better sign off.

Love

Daniel

'Well, mate, this it! I'll see you in Jerry's trenches soon.'

'See you there, cobber,' responded Frankie.

Fromelles Trench

They heard the whistle and the officer close to them yelled: 'Give them hell boys! Over you go!'

Daniel and Frankie clambered over the top and started to run, heading for Sugar Loaf, their objective, according to orders.

Machine Guns were firing from all directions. Daniel could hear the bullets tearing through the flesh of the Diggers running beside him. He found a shell crater and jumped in, only to find three bodies lying in the water at the bottom.

'So this is what they call ANZAC soup,' he thought.

He knew he could not stay there long so he clambered up the slope and was starting to run again. He had not fired a shot yet… a bit useless from this far away.

He looked around to see if Frankie was still near him; he was.

'Frankie, over here, mate.'

Frankie ran in a crouching motion and dropped down next to his cobber.

'Fuck, this is unbelievable mate! How the fuck are we gunna take out Sugar Loaf?'

'I think I can do it, mate. Give me your grenades. Right, I want you to cover me while I crawl to the base of this big ugly bastard. If I can get close enough without getting a bullet up the arse, I'll throw these babies in.'

Daniel could feel his heart pumping against his chest and he was secreting a cold sweat. He told himself with conviction, 'you can do this, mate.'

He pulled himself along the rough ground, stopping when shells were coming dangerously close, then moving on again. He finally reached his target and pulled the pins on all three grenades at once. This was a very risky thing to do as the "Mills Bomb" only had a four second fuse.

He threw the first into Sugar Loaf, then the second and by the time the third was thrown, the first exploded. The second and third exploded soon after completely destroying the blockhouse's interior and its German occupants.

Daniel was showered in concrete and was taken back to the Dressing Station where his wounds were dressed then on to the base hospital where he convalesced for two weeks.

He was mentioned in all dispatches and was awarded a Victoria Cross.

The two best friends, Richard and Daniel ended up in the same hospital, one with V.D and the other a V.C.

All Aboard For
The Magical Mystery Tour
Chapter 20

Band on the Run

John White was licking his wounds after surviving the horrendous battles at
Mouquet Farm and Pozieres, France.

It had been an horrendous few weeks with many of his mates dying from
German shellfire and bullets.

The attack was launched on 23 July 1916; this was to become known as the
Battle of Pozieres Ridge. Australian and British forces fought hard for an area

that comprised a relatively high observation post over the surrounding countryside. There was also the additional benefit of offering an alternative approach to the rear of the Thiepval defences where the Germans were entrenched.

The Australian divisions of the 1st Anzac Corps, having served in Gallipoli, were primarily given the task of capturing Pozieres Ridge. This had been an objective for capture on the first day of the Somme Offensive. The Australians succeeded in capturing the ridge by 4 August, having launched their offensive almost two weeks earlier

The British 48th Division assisted them in the attack.

The Australian Diggers succeeded in capturing Pozieres village itself, after which they moved across the main road towards "Gibraltar", a German strongpoint. A mere two hundred yards separated the Australians from Pozieres Ridge, the attack's main objective, heavily defended by the securely entrenched German troops. Two lines of trenches needed to be overcome before the ridge could be claimed. This action created a heavy toll on the Australian and British troops.

Later on that first day, 23 July, the British 17th Warwickshire Regiment joined the Australians to the northwest of Pozieres village. The Germans weren't going anywhere; they defended the ridge valiantly.

The 2nd Australian Division subsequently relieved their comrades and continued the attack on the ridge for a further four days before they too were relieved. Allied casualties at this stage were running at a costly three thousand five hundred.

The ridge finally fell after almost two weeks of bitter fighting on 4th August. However, both Mouquet Farm and Thiepval remained under German control. General Gough insisted they take these two targets and persisted with this plan, resulting in twenty three thousand Australian casualties.Gough came under Australian criticism for his persistence in pushing the advance for five weeks; growing scepticism of the quality of British leadership had already intensified following the notable failure of an earlier Battle at Fromelles, west of Lille, on 19-20 July by the Australian 5th Division, intended to divert German attention away from the Somme.

During this battle, the Australians suffered five thousand, seven hundred and eight casualties, of which a total of four thousand were fatalities; a further four hundred were captured and marched by the Germans through Lille. Their lives as prisoners of war were about to begin.

John White was exhausted and fed up with what seemed to be futile battles and horrendous casualties. This was not what he had signed up for; he had left his mother and father and his little sister behind to try and look after the farm in East Gippsland, Victoria so he could go and fight for King and country. He didn't feel like he was doing that, he was fighting for bloody incompetent British Generals like Gough.

His good mate, Willy Jones, was lying on his back smoking his last cigarette before the Red Cross could deliver some more. Who knows when that would be?

'Mate, I'm sick of this fucking war! I reckon we should opt out, you know… piss off.'

'What are you talking about, Will? Ya can't just say, 'I've had enough of this shit, I'm out a here. Going home.'

'Why the fuck not? Plenty of others have pissed off.'

'You mean become a deserter? Where are we going to go?'

'The closest place would be Holland. It's not far and we can see out this fucking war wearing clogs and picking tulips.'

'I must admit that sounds a bloody lot better than being shot at by the Krauts.'

'How in the hell are we going to walk two hundred odd miles without being questioned?'

'I have been giving that some thought, Johnno..'

'Well that's good! I'm glad you have been planning our escape. What have you come up with?'

'I reckon we should steal one of the troop buses and simply drive up there.'

'Mate, that's easier said than done. If we do manage to pinch a bus, surely the officers along the way are going to question why there's only two bloody privates on the bus!'

'Mate, I've been planning this escape for some time; I've already recruited eight other Diggers to come along. You're the last to be approached.'

'Why am I the last?'

'Cause I knew you would be the hardest to recruit but with ten of us committed, you might come along.'

'You're right! I'm in. So, who else is coming?'

'Jimmie Taylor, George Brown, Charlie Wilson, Bob Williams, Joe Robinson,

Frank Johnston, Eddie, Tom Smith and Henry Andersen.'

'Jeez, mate, it's quite a group you've banded together.'

'When do we go?'

While there's a lull in the fighting, like now.'

'You mean today?'

'Why not? There's a couple of the double deckers parked in Pozieres at the moment.'

'OK, are all the other boys aware of the plan?'

'Yep, ready to go… just waiting for the word.'

Willy and Johnno rounded up the rest of the would- be deserters and walked into the village. This didn't arouse suspicions, as it was quite normal for soldiers to visit Pozieres.

They spotted a bus parked outside the hotel. Willy looked inside the cabin; the keys were in the ignition. He climbed inside and signalled the others to board. He started her up and off they drove. Nobody in the street batted an eyelid. It all looked perfectly normal.

Off to Holland We Go

They had been driving on pock- marked roads for about an hour when they came across a platoon of British soldiers; the Captain in charge waved them down.

'Where are you chaps off to?'

John spoke up.

'We are heading for the Dutch border, Sir. Our orders are to pick up ten escaped POWs and bring them back to Ypres.'

'Oh, that's no good to us. We're heading in the opposite direction. I thought we might be able to hitch a lift. On your way.'

Willie drove off and everybody started to breathe again.

They drove on without incident and only stopped for a toilet break three hours into the journey. They reached the Dutch border and drove into neutral territory and were soon in the beautiful town of Maastricht.

Willie pulled up outside the oldest pub in town, "In Den Ouden Vogelstruys" (In The Old Ostrich). The deserters entered to have a celebratory pint and discuss their plans.

'So, what in the fuck do we do now cobbers?' asked Jimmie Taylor.

'Well, the first thing we do is find a photographer and get a photo of the gang so we can post it back to the commander.' This they did.

'Au revoir, Nous 'us'.

The message on the postcard infuriated Sir Harold Walker who was leading the Australian troops very effectively: overall, he was very proud of the Australian troops.

The next thing was to decide what to do with "Old Betsy', the bus.

'We can't just bloody drive around in her all day. That would bring all sorts of attention; we don't need that,' said Joe Robinson.

'I've already thought about that,' Will answered.'I reckon we put a For Sale sign on her near the main square. Bet ya she'll sell as quick as a flash.'

'Well, it's worth a go; we could do with the bloody dosh,' said Frank.'How much do ya reckon we could get for the old girl, Will?'

'Oh I dunno, maybe fifty quid.'

'You're kidding! Fifty quid? Really?

'Yeah, not too many buses like her around these parts; somebody will buy it.'

They made up a sign for both front and back and parked her near the main square. They took it in turns to babysit her and answer any questions potential buyers may have.

On the third day, a large gentleman approached John, who was on bus duty.

'How much do you want for the bus, soldier?'

'Fifty pounds.'

'Fifty pounds; is she made from gold?'

'Worth every penny, squire. She goes like a trooper.'

'I'll give you thirty pounds.'

'Make it forty and she's yours.'

'Do you have ownership papers?'

'All right, make it thirty five.'

'Thirty.'

'Done.'

The man handed over the thirty pounds and John walked down the street with more money in his pockets than he had ever had before.

He reached the pub where they all met at five in the evening every night and handed over the money to their leader, Will.

'Where's the other twenty pounds, Johnno?

'That's the best I could do. He was asking about ownership papers and stuff.'

'OK, thirty quid is better than nothing. That means we each get three quid, boys. Sounds like a lot but it's got to last until we can all find a way to earn some more. It's not going to be easy finding a job here, not speaking the language and all.'

How You Going to Keep Them Down on the Farm?

Chapter 21

Frank and Tom were farm boys who had never known any other life. They decided they would leave Maastricht and head for the country to try and find some farm work. They stumbled on a town called Beers, which appealed to them immediately. They entered a small pub and, after several beers, asked the barman if he knew of any farms that could use experienced farm hands. He directed them to the De Jong farm just three kilometres down the road. On arrival, they asked a young fellow on a horse-drawn cart where they could find farmer De Jong. He directed them to the farmhouse and they proceeded to knock on the front door.

A big bearded man appeared.

'What do you want?' he said abruptly.

'We were just wondering if you could use two very experienced farm hands, sir?'

'Can you erect a fence?'

'Yes, sir,' they replied, both at once.

'Can you operate a plough?'

'Absolutely.'

'Have you worked with cattle?'

'For many years.'

'Where are you from?'

'Australia.'

'Why aren't you fighting the Germans in Belgium?'

'We got caught behind German lines. We had no choice but to flee to Holland,' explained Frank.

'Okay, I'll give you some work; you'll have to sleep in the barn. Start tomorrow at seven o'clock.'

'Thank you, Mr De Jong. Can we sleep in the barn tonight?'

'I suppose so.'

The next morning the Australian deserters were waiting outside the farmhouse for Mr De Jong. At seven o'clock he opened the door and greeted them with a nod. 'Come with me,' he said, as he strode off towards one of the farm's outbuildings. Inside the shed were a tractor and a trailer.

'Have either of you ever driven one of these things?'

'Yes, sir, we used them on our farms back home,' Tom assured the farmer.

Frank and Tom and the De Jong Tractor

Farmer De Jong started up his pride and joy; they headed out to the wheat paddocks at the far end of the property. Mr De Jong drove and the boys sat in the trailer behind.

Once they arrived at the designated field, they rigged up the plough.

'I'll plough the first rows then you can show me how good you both are.'

Frank was the first to give it a go; it was obvious he had ploughed using a tractor before. Tom also proved his dexterity. Satisfied with their skills, Mr De Jong left them to plough the remainder of the field while he went off to do other things.

At the end of the day, Frank and Tom parked the tractor they had nick- named "Matilda" back in the shed.

At six o'clock Mrs De Jong delivered their dinner to the barn. Mr De Jong had cleared an area at the back of the building and installed a table and chairs and two single beds. Washing was done at the pump just outside the barn door. It was pretty rudimentary but comfortable.

Frank and Tom enjoyed their time at the De Jong farm and Mr De Jong enjoyed having them there to help. The harvest was the best the farm had produced and the profitability of the farm had risen significantly.

After six months of living in the barn, the boys moved into a cottage De Jong had constructed along with the Australians' help. On Sundays they were invited to join the family for a roast dinner. The De Jongs had a thirteen-year-old son, Hans, and two daughters, Anika, aged twenty and Helena, aged nineteen.

The Sunday night dinner became the highlight of the week with stories from Australia being told and the history of Europe being discussed. Rarely would the European war be mentioned.

Frank and Tom taught Hans how to play Australian Rules, albeit with a soccer ball, not the traditional egg- shaped ball the game was normally played with. Hans became quite skilled at kicking the ball and marking.

By the time the war ended in November 1918, the boys were well and truly entrenched into the De Jong family. Frank was engaged to Anika and Tom to Helena.

They never returned to their homeland. They married and raised a family, working and expanding the De Jong farm.

Stowaways

Chapter 22

Will and John had decided that the best option for them would be to get to Ireland somehow, wait out the war and eventually get back home.

Great plan, but how were they going to achieve it?

'Mate, how much money have you got left?'

'Two pounds, Will, what about you?'

'About the same.'

'I think that's going to be enough. We don't have to buy tickets, in fact we can't: we don't have identity papers.'

'Yeah, so we need to stow away on a ship to England.'

'The first thing we need to do is get to a major port and find the right ship.'

John did some investigation and discovered the port city of Flushing was not only the nearest, it was the port used for trade between England and Holland.

The two adventurers prepared to leave, saying goodbye to the rest of the lads. Their plan was to catch a bus, which would take them about three hours and cost fifty pence.

The bus trip was uneventful; both of them enjoyed seeing the fields of tulips and the traditional windmills along the way.

The bus stopped at the wharves where they stepped off into a bustling port with ships being loaded with their cargo while others were being unloaded.

The stowaways just watched, trying to determine what ships were heading for England and what ships were going further abroad. Through serendipity they overheard two men talking about a ship that left every morning for England; the name of the ship was "Mecklenbury".

The two men walked to the dock where the ship was due to depart but it wasn't there. It had already been loaded and was anchored out about two hundred metres, ready to sail at seven am the next morning.

Neither of them was a strong swimmer, so that option wasn't open to them. The only real option was to steal a dinghy and row out in the dead of night.

They went into the town and found a nice restaurant where they could eat their last Dutch meal.

At twelve midnight they started to search for a suitable vessel and they hopped into one, only to find the oars had been removed. After searching for an hour, they found a dinghy with its oars and it was not padlocked to its mooring. It was much further from the ship than the first one but it was available.

John and Will climbed in and started to row; the current was strong and going against them,which made for difficult rowing. Exhausted, they arrived at the "Mecklenbury" where their plan was to climb the anchor chain, get aboard and find a suitable place to hide.

John clambered up first, with Will in close pursuit; John peered over the ship's railing and couldn't see anybody: they were in luck.

The two stowaways quietly moved across the deck, keeping a sharp eye out for any crew members. John spotted a lifeboat about twenty metres ahead.

'Will, let's get into the life- boat. Nobody will look for us there,'

John whispered.

'Okay, mate.'

They reached the boat, undid the ropes, pulled back the tonneau cover and slipped inside.

'Will, we can't speak, not even in whispers until we're safely in London. Okay?'

'Okay.'

Unbeknown to the two stowaways, a crewmember in the shadows had been watching them since they climbed on board.

They had been in the boat for about five minutes when the tonneau cover was pulled open. A tall blonde Nordic type was standing there with a revolver in his hand pointing it at the two Diggers.

'Who are you and why are you attempting to stow away?'

John and Will explained their predicament as best they could.

'I'll make a deal with you. You both give me one pound and I will pull the cover back and help you get off the ship tomorrow morning. Or, if you like, I can take you to the captain and he can decide what to do with you.'

They both agreed that the deal seemed very reasonable and handed over the money.

Sleeping on the floor of a lifeboat proved to be difficult but eventually both of them got some sleep.

They awoke to the ship's horn announcing their arrival at Canary Wharf.

True to his word, the big blonde fellow got them off the ship bypassing customs.

They were free to walk the streets of London with fifty pence in their pockets.

Knowing there was no way they could get to Ireland with only fifty pence they decided to try and get to Nottingham, where John had an Uncle who ran a steel mill.

They did make it with a few pennies left. They both got a job with the steel mill, no questions asked. Labour was scarce and the mill was running at full capacity to keep up with the war effort.

In 1920, both John and Will boarded a ship bound for Sydney, Australia. They had been exonerated of any misdeeds.

Military Refugees

Chapter 23

Harderwijk Camp

The other Australian deserters, having run out of money, handed themselves in to the Dutch authorities. The Dutch had established camps to house not only genuine refugees from the war but also thousands of deserters from all countries including Germany.

Jim Taylor, Charles Wilson, Robert Williams, Joseph Robinson, Frank Johnston, Edward Martin - all became guests of the Netherlands at Harderwijk Camp.

In an area of thirty-two hectares, there were fifty barracks built where twelve to fifteen thousand interned could be accommodated. Harderwijk Camp was designed as a small village with schools, shops, bath houses, canteens, churches, post offices, etc.

The deserters spent the duration of the war here, enjoying a reasonably comfortable life.

After six months, the Aussie Diggers were regarded as trusted detainees and permitted to work outside the camp under supervision. Jo and Ed worked at the wharf in Rotterdam, loading and unloading ships. It was not unlike the work they did back in Melbourne before the war. Jimmie and Charlie worked in the coal mine at South Limburg and Frank and Charlie laboured on a local farm.

When travelling to Rotterdam, Ed and Joe would pass the women's camp at Lopold's Dorp. They could see very attractive young women who would often smile and wave at the detainees as they passed in an open truck. Boys will be boys and the Aussies couldn't restrain the testosterone flooding through their veins.

Female Camp

They devised a scheme where they would escape at night through an undetected weak point in the perimeter fence and make their way to the women's camp. Initially they waited outside the fence, hoping to spot the women they had seen on their trips to the port. Eventually they decided they needed to take the risk and write notes, wrap them around a rock and throw them over the fence, hoping it would be a detainee and not a guard that would find them.

They needed to return the next night to see if their plan had worked. They crept up to the fence and waited. Sure enough two young Belgian women were waiting for them; through broken English they explained where the two Diggers could enter the camp undetected. Ed and Joe slithered under the wire on their bellies without much difficulty; the two girls beckoned them to follow them. They entered a wooden building, which was used as a gymnasium; passing all the Gym equipment, they entered the dressing room. The four had hardly spoken but as soon as they entered the room both girls grabbed the boys and kissed them passionately. There was no doubt in any one's mind why they were here together in the dressing room of a Gym in a women's detention camp in Holland.

Both girls unbuttoned their prison tunics and lowered them down to the waist, they then unhooked their bras allowing the boys to fondle their ample breasts and kiss their nipples.

Both girls looked at each other, smiled and nodded, then both went down on their knees and commenced undoing their belts and unbuttoning flies. They took the soldiers in their mouths and began to suck, lick and kiss their erect penises.

Joe and Ed couldn't contain themselves, grabbing the girls, placing them on the change benches and fucking to the point of exhaustion.

The boys agreed to return in a week and make it a weekly rendezvous until either the war was over or they got transferred to another camp.

The two exhausted soldiers made their way back safely to their own camp without incident. When they were back in the barracks they started to laugh.

'What a fucking night, Joe! Can you believe it?'

'Mate, that was the best I've ever had, not that I've had many.'

'Do ya know what?'

'What.'

'I don't even know her name.'

'Me neither.'

'Well we better introduce ourselves next time.'

'Yeah I suppose we should.'

Jim and Charlie had no such luck, they were transported by truck to the coalfields at South Limburg six days a week, where they worked underground for ten hours a day without pay.

Frank and Charlie worked on a farm quite close to the De Jong farm although they had no idea that they were virtually neighbours with Frank and Tom. After one year working on the farm of Mr and Mrs Bargen, they were granted leave from the camp and resided in workers' huts on the property. When the war finally ended, the six Australians were repatriated back to Australia without penalty.

The Red Baron

Chapter 24

Manfred Albrecht von Richthofen was born on May 2, 1892, the first-born son. His father, Major Albrecht Freiherr von Richthofen was extremely proud and decided Manfred would follow him into the military even though he couldn't walk yet. Two more sons, Lothar and Karl Bolko, soon followed.

The Richthofens came from a long aristocratic line that could be traced back to the sixteenth century. Manfred grew up in his family's villa in the town of Schweidnitz. His Uncle Alexander, an avid hunter, who had hunted in Africa, Asia and Europe, encouraged Manfred to hunt.

Manfred's father , Albrecht, had become one of the first Richthofens' to join the military and become a career officer.

Albrecht's retirement from the army was premature; he had gone deaf as a result of rescuing several comrades from the icy Oder River.

Manfred did follow his chosen career; when eleven years old, Manfred entered the Wahlstatt cadet school in Berlin. He did not warm to the discipline and as a result his grades were quite poor. Where he did excel was in athletics and gymnastics. After six not particularly happy years at Wahlstatt, Manfred graduated to the Senior Cadet Academy at Lichterfelde, which he found more to his liking. After completing a course at the Berlin War Academy, Manfred joined the cavalry.

In 1912, Manfred, was commissioned as Leutnant (lieutenant), he was stationed at Militsch.

In July 1914, World War I began.

Manfred was twenty-two years old and stationed on Germany's eastern border. It didn't take long for him to be transferred to The Western Front. During the invasion of Belgium and France, Manfred's cavalry regiment was attached to the infantry and Manfred conducted reconnaissance patrols.

When it became obvious that cavalry were not needed in the trenches, Manfred was transferred to the Signal Corps. His role was to lay telephone wires and deliver dispatches.

Richthofen did not enjoy life in the trenches although he enjoyed better conditions than the British. The German trenches were still damp and infested with rats but better built.

He loved observing the planes overhead conducting their reconnaissance missions. He decided this was going to be his new role, however, he also knew that to become a pilot took months of training and by the time he qualified, the war would be over, or so he thought.

Richthofen requested a transfer to the Air Service to become an observer. In May 1915, Richthofen travelled to Cologne for the observer-training program at the number seven Air Replacement Station. Manfred recalled his first flight:

'At seven o'clock the next morning I was to fly for the first time as an observer. Naturally, I was very excited, because I could not imagine what it would be like. Everyone I asked told me something different. The night before, I had gone to bed earlier than usual to be fresh for the great moment next morning. We drove to the airfield and I sat in an airplane for the first time. The blast of wind from the propeller disturbed me greatly. It was impossible to make myself heard by the pilot. Everything flew away from me. If I took a piece of paper out, it disappeared. My flying helmet slipped off, my muffler loosened too much, and my jacket was not buttoned securely - in short, I was miserable. Before I knew what was happening, the pilot got the engine up to full speed and the machine began rolling, faster and faster. I hung on frantically. Then the shaking stopped and we were in the air. The ground slipped away beneath us.'

During this first flight, Richthofen became disoriented and was unable to give the pilot directions. When they landed, the pilot castigated the young recruit and stormed off. Richthofen continued his training. He was taught how to read a map, drop bombs, locate enemy troops, and draw pictures while still in the air - no easy task.

Richthofen passed observer training and was sent to the Eastern Front where his assignment was to report enemy troop movements. After several months of flying as an observer in the East, Manfred was ordered to report to the "Mail Pigeon Detachment," the code name for a new secret unit.

Richthofen had his first dogfight on September 1, 1915. He was flying with Lieutenant Georg Zeumer when Manfred spotted an enemy aircraft, his first. Richthofen had only a rifle with him and though he tried several times to hit the other plane, he failed to bring it down.

A few days later, Richthofen went up again, this time with Lieutenant Osteroth. Armed with a machine gun, Richthofen fired at the enemy plane but unfortunately the gun jammed. Richthofen unjammed the gun and fired again. The enemy plane started to spiral and eventually crashed into the field. Richthofen was elated.

On October 1 1915, Richthofen was on board a train heading for Metz. After entering the dining car, he found an empty, seat sat down and noticed a familiar face at another table. Richthofen introduced himself and found that he was talking to the famous fighter pilot, Lieutenant Oswald Boelcke.

Boelcke

Frustrated with his ability to shoot down another plane, Richthofen asked 'Boelcke, 'Tell me honestly, how do you really do it?'

Boelcke laughed and replied., 'Good heavens, it indeed is quite simple. I fly in as close as I can, take good aim, shoot, and then he falls down.'

Though Boelcke hadn't given Richthofen the answer he had hoped for, it gave Manfred something to think about. Richthofen realised the new single seater Fokker fighter, the one that Boelcke flew, was much easier to shoot from.

Richthofen asked his friend, Zeumer, to teach him to fly. After many lessons, Zeumer agreed with Richthofen that he was ready for his first solo flight.

'There are few moments in life that produce as nervous a sensation as the first solo flight. Zeumer, my teacher, announced to me one afternoon: "You are ready to fly alone." I must say that I would rather have answered: "I am too afraid." But this could never come from a defender of the fatherland. Therefore, good or bad, I had to swallow my cowardice and sit in the machine... The engine started with a roar. I gave it the gas and the machine began to pick up speed, and suddenly I could not help but notice that I was really flying. Suddenly it was no longer an anxious feeling, but, rather, one of daring. Now it was all up to me. No matter what happened, I was no longer frightened.'

Richthofen passed all three of the fighter pilot examinations. On December 25, 1915, he was awarded his pilot's certificate. He had never before received such a wonderful Christmas present.

Richthofen spent the next several weeks with the 2nd Fighting Squadron near Verdun in France. Richthofen engaged several enemy planes and shot one down, however he wasn't credited with the kill because the plane went down in enemy territory with no witnesses.

The squadron was transferred to the Eastern Front where they were ordered to bomb the Russian troops.

When returning from Turkey in August 1916, Oswald Boelcke visited his brother, Wilhelm, Richthofen's commander. Apart from family business, Boelcke was scouting for pilots with talent. Boelcke invited Richthofen and one other pilot to join his new group called "Jagdstaffel 2" "hunting squadron" in Lagnicourt, France.

'Suddenly in the early morning, there was a knock at the door and before me stood the great man with the Pour le Mérite. I really did not know what he wanted of me. To be sure, I knew him . . . but it did not occur to me that he had sought me out to invite me to become a pupil of his. I could have hugged him when he asked whether I wanted to go to the Somme with him.'

By September 8 1916, Richthofen had arrived in Lagnicourt. Boelcke then taught them all he knew about aerial combat.

'We were all beginners; none of us had previously been credited with a success. Whatever Boelcke told us was taken as gospel. We knew that in the last few days he had shot down at least one Englishman a day, and many times two every morning. . . . We approached the enemy squadron slowly, but it could no longer escape us. We were between the Front and the enemy. If he wanted to go back, he would have to go by us. We counted seven enemy airplanes, and opposed them with only five. . . . The Englishman near me was a big, dark-coloured barge. I did not ponder long and took aim at him. He shot and I shot, but we both missed. The fight then began. I tried to get behind him because I could only shoot in the direction I was flying. This was not necessary for him, as his observer's rotating machine gun could reach all sides. But this fellow was no beginner, for he knew very well that the moment I succeeded in getting behind him, his

last hour would be sounded. At the time I did not have the conviction I have now that "he must fall," but, rather, I was much more anxious to see if he would fall, and that is a significant difference. . . . '

The propeller on the British plane had stopped rotating; the engine had been shot and destroyed. The enemy would have to land behind German lines where Manfred would get an opportunity to meet his foe.

The enemy airplane landed and Richthofen, extremely excited about his first kill, landed his airplane next to his enemy's. The observer, Lieutenant T. Rees, was already dead and the pilot, L. B. F. Morris died on the way to hospital.

It was Richthofen's first credited victory. He was presented with an engraved beer mug, as was the custom between the fliers when they had achieved their first kill

This gave Richthofen an idea. To celebrate each of his victories, he would order himself a two-inch-high silver trophy from a jeweller in Berlin. On his first cup was engraved, "1 VICKERS 2 17.9.16." The first number reflected what number was the kill; the word represented what kind of airplane; the third item represented the number of crew on board; and the fourth was the date of the victory (day, month, year).

The Red Baron in Full Flight

As he became more successful, Richthofen decided to make every tenth victory cup twice as large as the others. As with many pilots, to remember his kills, Richthofen became an avid souvenir collector. After shooting down an enemy aircraft, Richthofen would land near it or drive to find the wreckage after the battle and take something from the plane. A few of his souvenirs included a machine gun, bits of propeller, even an engine. But most commonly, Richthofen removed the fabric serial numbers from the aircraft. He would carefully pack up these souvenirs and send them home to be placed in his room.

In the beginning, each new kill was exciting, however later in the war Richthofen's kills had a sobering effect. When it came time to order his sixty-first silver trophy, the jeweller in Berlin informed him that due to a scarcity of silver, he would have to use a substitute. Richthofen decided to end his trophy collecting.

On October 28, 1916, Boelcke took to the air the air as he did on most days. During an aerial battle, a horrible accident occurred. While trying to evade an enemy, Boelcke and another German plane collided. Though it was only a touch, Boelcke's plane was damaged; Boelcke's plane plummeted towards the ground when one of his wings snapped off.

Boelcke was killed on impact.

The German people were mortified; their greatest hero had been killed. Who would replace him?

The norm had been when a fighter pilot registered nine kills, he would receive Germany's highest award; The Blue Max. Manfred reached the number only to discover the requisite number of kills had risen to sixteen. Richthofen's success in the air started to make him known to the German people as well as the military hierarchy.

Richthofen decided he would make himself even better known; some pilots had colourfully painted their wings or their propellers, but Richthofen decided he would paint his entire plane bright red. No one else would be so audacious. Now people on the ground and the enemy in the air would know he was there.

> 'One day, for no particular reason, I got the idea to paint my crate glaring red. After that, absolutely everyone knew my red bird. If fact, even my opponents were not completely unaware.'

Richthofen knew the red plane put fear into his enemies, although some pilots thought it made a good target. There was a rumour circulating that the British had put a price on the red plane's pilot. The red plane and its pilot continued to shoot down British planes and soon earned the respect of their adversaries.

The British and French created nicknames for Richthofen: Le Petit Rouge, the Red Devil, the Red Falcon, Le Diable Rouge, the Jolly Red Baron, the Bloody Baron, and the Red Baron. However, the Germans never called Richthofen the Red Baron; instead, they called him der röte Kampfflieger ("The Red Battle Flier").

Richthofen was awarded the Blue Max on January 12, 1917. Two days later, he was given command of Jagdstaffel 11. Now he was not only to fly and fight, but also to train others to do so.

April 1917 was titled "Bloody April." After several months of rain and cold, the weather improved and pilots from both Germany and Britain took to the air. The Germans had the advantage in both location and aircraft. In April, Richthofen shot down twenty-one enemy aircraft, bringing his total to fifty-two. He had finally broken Boelcke's record of forty victories making Richthofen the new "ace of aces".

Manfred was a hero; postcards were printed with his image and stories of his prowess abounded. Yet heroes in war don't necessarily last long. Any day the hero might not come home. The war planners wanted to protect the German hero and thus they ordered him to rest.

Leaving his brother Lothar in charge of Jasta 11, Richthofen departed on May 1, 1917 to visit Kaiser Wilhelm II. He talked to many of the top generals, spoke to youth groups, and socialized.

During his sabbatical, the war planners and propagandists had asked Richthofen to write his memoirs. He did so and they were later published as Der Rote Kampfflieger ("The Red Battle-Flyer"). By mid June, Richthofen was back with his comrades at Jasta 11.

In June 1917, the air wings were combined to create one large formation named Jagdgeschwader I ("Fighter Wing 1") Richthofen was to be the commander. This became known as "The Flying Circus"

July 1917

British RE8

Richthofen was flying a mission with five of his squadron over the fields of Northern France; the day was perfect for hunting and the Germans were on the lookout for British fighters. Richthofen caught a glimpse of a plane from the corner of his eye. It was a solitary British bomber; an RE8. These planes were great bombers but no match in a dogfight for the German Albatrosses. The Red Baron increased altitude with his squadron following; they swooped out of the glaring sun and opened fire. All six planes ripped into the British plane but failed to shoot it down. They circled and came back with their lethal guns firing. The plane was in tatters with most of its canvas cover missing. Still, it flew on and the Germans again strafed the British fortress.

Finally the British plane decided to land on a nearby German airfield. The landing was perfect. Richthofen and his fellow pilots also landed and ran over to the enemy plane. They could not believe what they saw; the pilot and his observer were riddled with bullets and very much dead! They counted three hundred bullets in each man.

Soon after, The Red Baron was engaged in a dogfight over France when he received a bullet to the head.

'Suddenly there was a blow to my head! I was hit! For a moment I was completely paralysed [sic] . . . My hands dropped to the side, my legs dangled inside the fuselage. The worst part was that the blow on the head had affected my optic nerve and I was completely blinded. The machine dived down.'

Richthofen regained partial eyesight at around eight hundred metres; despite his head wound, he was able to land his plane. He remained on leave until August, although he continued to suffer severe headaches for the rest of his life

By April 1918 the war was beginning to turn in favour of Britain and her allies. Richthofen was losing his enthusiasm for war and death. The Red Baron had nothing to prove either to himself or his country as he was close to registering his eightieth victory, twice as many as Boelcke. His headaches caused him great discomfort and he lapsed into periods of depression. Despite this, he refused his superior's requests to retire.

The day started just like any other. The Red Baron climbed into his bright red plane to lead a challenge to a group of British aircraft which had been sighted near the front. The date was April 21, 1918.

Leading from the front, Richthofen spotted the British planes and the fight began. The Baron saw a single plane fly off out of the melee; he followed it, determined to shoot it down. The young pilot was Canadian Second Lieutenant Wilfred ("Wop") May.

The Germans spotted the British planes and a battle ensued. Richthofen noticed a single airplane bolt out of the melee. Richthofen followed him. Inside the British plane sat Canadian Second Lieutenant Wilfred ("Wop") May. This was May's first combat flight and his superior, Canadian Captain Arthur R. Brown, was keeping a lookout for his young protégé. May's guns jammed and he tried to make a dash for home.

To the Red Baron, May looked like an easy kill and pursued him. Captain Brown noticed the Baron's bright red plane chasing his friend. He knew who the pilot was and decided to break away from the battle and try to help his friend.

May realised he was being pursued and from the plane's red colour, he knew it was The Red Baron; he was petrified.

May flew close to the ground, skimming over the tree tops, and over the Morlancourt Ridge. Richthofen anticipated the move and swung around to cut May off.

Captain Brown had now caught up and started firing at Richthofen. As the three planes passed over the ridge, Australian Diggers fired up at the German plane. Richthofen was hit. Everyone watched as the bright red plane crashed.

Once the ANZACs had reached the fallen plane, they realised it was The Red Baron. They ravaged the plane, taking pieces as souvenirs. Not much was left by the time the British investigators arrived on the crash scene. It was determined that a single bullet had entered through the right side of Richthofen's back and exited about two inches higher from his left chest. The bullet killed him instantly. He was twenty-five years old.

There is still conjecture as to who actually brought Richthofen down

Was it Captain Brown or was it one of the Australian soldiers?

We will never know.

Baron Manfred von Richthofen, the Red Baron, was credited with bringing down eighty enemy aircraft. His prowess in the air made him a German hero during World War I and he was famous forever more.

Poperinge Revisited

Chapter 25

Parts from Richthofen's Plane

The remains of Baron von Richthofen's Fokker Triplane were kept at the aerodrome of No. 3 Squadron, Australian Flying Corps.

Harry Andersen had been on the front for over eighteen months during which he had been wounded, seduced and seen plenty of carnage; he was now regarded as a very capable gunner using his Vickers machine gun with great skill.

He was sitting around with his mates as he often did, waiting for some action.

Suddenly Harry shouted:

> 'Well fuck me, look at that.'

'Look at what, Harry?'

'Up there, a dog fight; two of our boys and one red plane.'

'Red plane!'

'That's the fucking Red Baron, they reckon he's killed more of our fliers than any other German bastard.'

'Holy hell!'

They watched in awe; the British plane was ducking and weaving, trying to lose the red plane. It flew low over the forest at the back of them and swerved up into the clouds. The Red Baron was firing continually and kept close to the tail of his adversary. Another British plane was following, firing at the back of the red plane and trying to protect his comrade.

Harry ran to his Vickers and started shooting at the German plane; three other gunners joined him. The planes passed low overhead. Harry and the boys let go a barrage of bullets at the Baron. The red plane started to fly erratically and plummeted to the earth. They all ran over and looked in the cockpit where the pilot, Baron Manfred Richthofen, other wise known as the "Red Baron", was dead. He was removed immediately and taken away for burial.

The Australians felt they had earned the right to strip Richthofen's plane in the hope of selling parts as souvenirs.

It didn't take long; they even grabbed the plane's engine.

By the time the military investigators arrived on the scene, it was merely a shell.

The Australian gunners felt quite pleased with themselves and even though the flier in the third plane, Captain Brown claimed the historic kill, they all knew it was one of them.

The four Diggers were given three days' leave and there was no doubt where they were heading: Poperinge or 'Pops' as they called it.

They took as much as they could of the Red Baron's tri-plane in their backpacks and headed for the playground.

They boarded 'Old Bill', the London Bus, and headed off.

When they arrived, Harry suggested they do the rounds of the pubs to see if they could sell the Red Baron's souvenirs. This they did and it didn't take long before most of the artefacts were sold for very good prices. They met at Talbot House to tally up the takings. They had managed to raise one hundred francs, a sizeable amount by their standards.

'What are we gunna do with all this money, fellas?' asked Billy.

'Dunno, we could go down to the pub and drink it.'

'I've got a better idea. Why don't we get the fucking Red Baron
to shout us all a romp in the hay at Madame Fifi's?' suggested Harry.

'Now ya talking Harry! Let's blow it at Maison de Plaisir.'

The four Australian gunners left Talbot House and headed down the road to Maison de Plaisir and some damn good hanky panky.

Madame Fifi was on the front desk as usual and welcomed the Aussie soldiers with a wide smile and a significant cleavage.

'Hello boys. So you are looking for some fun with my beautiful
girls?'

'That's right Madame we would all like an hour, please.' Billie
told her.

'That will be five francs each.'

'That seems reasonable, Madame. Is there much of a wait?'

'I am afraid there is, it is very busy tonight.'

'Oh well, not much you can do about that is there?'

'If you were able to pay another two francs each, I should be able to lessen your wait.'

'What do you reckon, boys?'

'Yeah, why not? Let's pay the extra dosh,' exclaimed Frankie, the youngest.

They paid the money and Madame Fifi led them to a private room at the back of the house.

'Hey, Madame, we all thought we would have our own room. Are you telling us we have to share?'

'Cheri, you will have an experience of a lifetime, just like a Roman orgy. Normally you would pay a lot more for this. If you do not wish to share, I will refund your extra payment and you can go and wait on the stairs along with all the other soldiers.'

'Can you just give us a minute to talk it over, Madame?'

'Of course, why not, but don't take too long. I need to get back to reception.'

'Well, cobbers, what do you think?'

'Geez, I dunno, it could be good.'

'I'm not sure if I want to see all your hairy arses bobbing up and down. It could be a bit off – putting,' complained Jimmie.

'Well, I reckon it's worth a go,' said Billie.

'OK let's do it.'

'Madame Fifi we have decided to go ahead.'

'You won't regret it, boys. You just wait here and I will send in the girls.'

The young soldiers waited, not talking much. The anticipation in the air was overpowering.

164

The door opened and Madame Fife led in the four girls. She introduced all four and then left them to it.

The soldiers just stood there, not knowing what the next step should be. They didn't have to worry; each of the girls approached one of the soldiers, took them by the hand and led them to one of the four double beds in the suite.

It wasn't too long before the eight people in the room were naked and enjoying themselves. It was a symphony of moans and groans and squeals. After about thirty minutes, Billie yelled: "OK, everybody, swap!"

No matter where they were in their lovemaking, they all moved over a place and started again. What bliss!

Finally their hour expired and Madame Fifi knocked loudly on the door to inform them all that they were out of time.

The soldiers dressed, having lost any inhibitions they might have had in the last hour.

They exited Maison de Plaisir in uncontrollably high spirits.

> 'Was that any good or not?' laughed Billie.
>
> 'Best fucking time I've ever had in my life. If I die tomorrow, I'll
> die happy,' said Frankie.

They sauntered down the pebbled street and decided to call in to a small pub on their way.

> 'You know what? Next time we're on leave I reckon we should
> do it again. What do ya reckon?'

They all agreed enthusiastically.

The next day they boarded one of the London buses and headed back to The Somme but as the bus turned a sharp corner, a German shell hit the bus square on, destroying the bus and all on board.

Frankie and his mates died happy.

Lost
Chapter 26

The two British Diggers were in the trench, that bloody horrible trench that had been home for too bloody long. They didn't know it at the time but they were taking part in the Kaiser's spring offensive. The Germans were throwing everything they could at the British and their allies, knowing full well that if this push did not succeed, the war would be lost. The Americans were landing in France in full force and shortly would be fighting shoulder to shoulder with the allies.

The bombardment had been going on for about six hours, a relentless barrage of fire and brimstone, when a British captain, Sam Wilson, approached the two comrades.

> 'Cook and Amos, I am asking you two to volunteer to go over the top when the blasted shells have stopped and try to determine when the German troops might be on our doorstep, as it were. It might give us a bit of notice to prepare a welcome for the blighters.'

Percy Cook and Tom Amos had been school friends and did everything together, including enlist. Why not embark together on this highly dangerous mission?

> 'I would like to volunteer, sir,' said Private Cook.

> 'I would like to also, sir,' Private Amos agreed.

> 'Right, well-done soldiers! I'll come back to you when I think the time is right for you to pop over.'

> 'Geez, mate, I hope we know what we're fucking doing.'

> 'Don't worry, Percy, she'll be right. If we see the Krauts coming, we just scurry down a big shell hole and play dead. They're not gunna

worry about a couple of dead Tommies down the bottom of a hole. Anyways, we'll high- tail it back to our line as soon as we smell the bastards.'

'Yeah, I guess you're right. As usual.'

'Make sure you bring some extra smokes and a can of bully beef; we might be out there for a while. We don't want to get stuck without the usual comforts.'

The Captain returned and gave them a last minute briefing and sent them on their way.

'Good luck, boys.'

Percy and Tom slowly climbed over the top; the craters from the German's artillery bombardment were everywhere, making it difficult to traverse no-man's land. They had reached to about two hundred yards from their own line, when Fritz opened up again for one last barrage. They kept their heads down and prayed they wouldn't end up as mincemeat as

they heard the whistle of a shell coming their way.

'Hit the fucking ground, quick!' shouted Percy.

They both were in the foetal position when the shell exploded; amazingly, shrapnel did not rip them apart. However, the force of the blast was so great that both lost consciousness. At about the same time, the German storm troopers started to attack, running past the two unconscious soldiers and breaking into the British line. The allies were forced into retreat, vacating their trenches.

At the end of the skirmish, the Germans had occupied the British fortifications; this left Percy and Tom behind enemy lines.

'What are we supposed to do now, mate? The fucking Krauts are in our trenches and our blokes have pissed off.'

'Yeah, I know. We really are up shit creek.'

167

'Well, the only thing to do is head in the opposite direction from where we are now.'

'You mean go deeper into Fritz's territory?'

'Mate, there's not gunna be too many Germans as they're all chasing our boys half way across bloody France.'

'So how's that gunna get us back with our lot?'

'Fucked if I know, but it should keep us alive long enough to work it out.'

'Yeah, well I suppose we don't have a lot options. Fuck it!'

The two Tommies crawled out of the shell crater and started to make their way across the apocalyptic landscape. They decided to stay clear of any roads or villages for the time being, where there could still be German troops on the ground or trucks bringing supplies to the front.

'Hey, Percy, what happens when we've eaten our rations? Where are we going to get our next feed?'

'Well, Tommy, I suppose we'll just have to steal some grub from an unsuspecting farmer or something. I dunno, we'll work it out.'

They trekked over the French countryside for about eight hours and were feeling the strain. They were both exhausted and needed some sleep.

'Hey Percy, we need to stop and get some rest. I really can't go much further.'

'Yeah, I know what ya mean mate; the trouble is, where can we lie down? We can't just drop where we stand... we'd stick out like dog's balls. We need to find a barn or something.'

'Let's go on a bit further in the hope we find a farm.'

The two weary soldiers walked for another thirty minutes when they spotted a farm in the distance.

'There, that fits the fucking bill. It's got a nice big barn and I'm sure plenty of hay to make ourselves a comfy bed.'

Gingerly they approached the barn and hoping not to attract any attention from the farmer, they slowly opened the barn door and peered inside. There were horses and cows and a couple of pigs.

'This is perfect, Tom! Come on, let's move right down the back.'

'Hey, mate, let's climb the ladder to the loft. Plenty of hay up there and we can't be easily spotted.'

'Beauty.'

They made themselves a cosy bed and were soon asleep.

They woke up to a large Frenchman with a fork in his hand prodding Percy's backside.

They didn't speak much French but understood what he was asking them: 'Who the fuck are you?'

'British.'

'Eh! Britannique? Pas allemand?' (Not German)

'Non! Non, Britannique'

The farmer helped them up and escorted them into the farmhouse. He explained to his family the two soldiers were British and instructed his wife to make them a hearty breakfast.

Although neither party spoke the other's language, they were able to communicate through drawings and hand gestures.

The family agreed to house the two soldiers until they could return somehow to their unit.

In the meantime, to earn their keep, they worked on the farm. They both picked up enough French to be able to communicate with the Babineaux family.

Tom and Percy worked hard, mending fences that had been destroyed by tanks and cutting and loading hay for winter-feed. They both enjoyed the work but knew they really should be back with their unit, fighting the bloody Germans. They also knew it was impossible to return, as the Germans had swept through and taken all the British territory.

They reconciled themselves to the fact they were here in Fontaine-Notre-Dame, either for the duration or until their boys pushed the Krauts back and re took the territory they had lost.

Antoine, the patriarch of the family approached the two boys.

'Messieurs, my neighbour would like you to help him mend some fencing. I will drive you over on the tractor.'

'That's fine, Monsieur. How long will we be staying there?' asked Percy.

'I would say two weeks, maybe three; you will like it there. He is a very nice man and his family is wonderful.'

The next morning Antoine drove the tractor the two miles to his neighbour's farm with the two soldiers sitting on the back wheel arches.

'Arnaud, these are the two British soldiers I told you about, Tom and Percy.'

'Pleased to meet you, Messieurs. I am sure you will be very happy working here.'

'Thank you. I am sure we will be very happy.'

'Ok, I'll leave you with Arnaud.'

Arnaud led them inside the farmhouse, which was much bigger than Antoine's and very old.

'Monsieur, how old is the house?'

'I believe it was built at the turn of the seventeenth century. It has been with my family for six generations.

'That's amazing; I take it is handed down from one generation to the next?' Tom asked.

'Oui, it is passed on to the first-born son.'

'Well, your son is very lucky.'

'Alas, I don't have a son, only three daughters.'

'So what happens? Does the eldest daughter inherit it?' asked Percy.

'Non, it will be sold when my wife and I retire.'

'Oh, I see.'

'Come, I'll show you your rooms.'

The two soldiers followed Arnaud to the loft on the third floor; each had his own room and they shared a bathroom.

'This is wonderful, monsieur, thank you!' exclaimed Tom.

'I am glad you like it; please call me Arnaud. When you settle in, we can go and look at the fences destroyed by the Germans.'

The two boys put their backpacks in their rooms and went downstairs to meet the rest of the family.

Arnaud's wife, Danielle, a very attractive woman in her early fifties. The three daughters were Elise aged twenty-one, Juliette aged nineteen and Margaux aged seventeen. They were all beautiful.

Arnaud could see the glint in the boys' eyes and knew he would have to manage his daughters very carefully while the British soldiers were there.

'Right, let's go and inspect the fences.'

He attached a large trailer to the tractor; both soldiers climbed on board and off they went. It took about fifteen minutes to reach the spot where Arnaud had decided to start the repairs.

It wasn't what the two boys expected; Antoine's fences were post and wire but these fences were dry rock walls. They knew nothing about stone!

'Arnaud, we have never worked with stone before and we don't know the first thing about stonewalls,' Percy apologised.

'Don't worry; I'm going to teach you. It's easy. As you can see, the tanks went straight through the walls but all the stone is still here.

So, at least we don't have to bring the stone in.'

Arnaud proceeded to teach them how to repair the wall using the correct sized stones at different levels.

They soon picked up the technique and, although it was hard work, they enjoyed the experience.

At day's end, they had repaired about ten metres of wall with a couple of hundred metres to go. It was around four o'clock when they headed back to the farmhouse; the regime was to wash up and join the family for a glass or two of wine and talk generally about how their day had gone. Occasionally they would talk about the war if some information had filtered through from the underground.

Dinner was always at six pm.

Danielle was a very good cook; she served a dish of rabbit in a cream sauce. All the ingredients came from the farm, where life was good for Percy and Tom; they worked hard, ate and drank well and behaved themselves with Arnaud and Danielle's daughters.

One day Juliette ran into the house screaming: 'Germans approaching the farm!'

It was five o'clock and they were enjoying a wine. They all jumped up and looked out the window. A car and two motorcycles were approaching at speed; they would be at the house in a few minutes.

Arnaud yelled to the soldiers.

'Quick, help me move the kitchen table! There is a trap door underneath.'

Percy and Tom did as they were instructed and scurried down the steep steps to a basement. Arnaud closed the trap door and he and his daughters moved the heavy table back. Elise had raced up to the loft and retrieved the boys' bags and clothes and toothbrushes and shavers from the bathroom. She raced downstairs and hid them in a wood box, placing logs over them.

Danielle grabbed the soldiers' wine glasses, hiding them in a cupboard. She hoped they wouldn't search the kitchen, as it was obvious they had been recently used.

The Germans knocked heavily on the front door. Arnaud opened it.

'Hello, I am Captain Bauer; we are checking all the farms in the area making sure there are no British soldiers being harboured. I ask you to be cooperative and we won't cause you or your family any harm.'

'Yes of course, Captain, please come in.'

The German Captain and four soldiers entered the farmhouse and proceeded to search all the rooms. After forty minutes of searching, they found nothing suspicious.

'We will now search your barn and the other outbuildings. If we find nothing, we will be on our way.'

The German contingent made a thorough search of the barn and departed.

Arnaud waited another hour to make completely sure the Germans had left and were not coming back.

The family moved the heavy oak table and opened up the door. Percy and Tom had been in complete darkness for over two hours and were well pleased to exit the cellar.

August 1918

Percy and Tom alternated between the two farms and were enjoying their time working on the land and establishing a friendship with both families.

It was a sunny autumn day; the boys were working on a fence near the farmhouse when once again, the call went out:

'Germans coming!'

Everybody dropped tools and ran for the farmhouse; luckily they were working on Arnaud's farm and therefore knew the routine. Once hidden in the cellar, they felt relatively safe. The two troop trucks pulled up outside and the British soldiers disembarked.

Arnaud welcomed them and informed the officer he had two British houseguests. The officer didn't seem that impressed.

'Where are they now?' enquired the officer, Lieutenant Hopwood.

'We hid them in the cellar as we thought you were the Germans returning,'

'So you've had Germans here, have you?'

'Yes, they were looking for British soldiers.'

'Well, so are we. Can you take me to them, please?'

Arnaud showed the Lieutenant and two soldiers into the kitchen, moved the table and opened the trap door.

'It is OK, boys; they are British. You are safe now.'

Percy and Tom emerged from the cellar and saluted the officer.

'How long have you two been staying here?'

'Since April, sir,' Percy explained.

'All right. Get your things and we'll get you back to HQ.'

The two British soldiers quickly grabbed their backpacks and their uniforms and accompanied the Lieutenant to the trucks. They didn't even get the opportunity to farewell the family.

When they arrived at HQ, they were escorted to the holding cells.

'What's going on? Why are we being locked up? We've done nothing wrong.'

'You are going to be questioned and if it is decided there is sufficient evidence, you will be court-martialled for desertion.'

'That's ridiculous. We didn't desert!'

'You will have ample opportunity to explain why you were behind enemy lines, working on a French farm.'

They were put in separate cells and told not to communicate; a guard was stationed at the end of the cellblock.

The next day Lieutenant Hopwood came to the cells and took Percy out for questioning. Percy explained the mission for which they had volunteered and how Captain Wilson signed the orders.

Next to be questioned was Tom; he also explained what had happened and corroborated Percy's story.

The Lieutenant was sceptical of the two soldiers' explanations, however he sought to verify the order with Captain Wilson. He made inquiries, only to discover that Captain Wilson had died in action only the week before. This would make it very difficult to verify the stories given by the two deserters. The decision was taken to proceed with the court martial.

The court martial lasted two hours only and Percy and Tom had no legal representation. They were found guilty of desertion and sentenced to death. Lieutenant Hopwood allowed the two boys to share a cell until the time of their execution. No date had yet been set.

'I can't fucking believe this, Tom! We do our fucking duty, put our lives at risk for King and fucking country and now the bastards are going to shoot us.'

'I know, Percy! There's no fucking justice in this world. Just think what Mum and Dad will go through back home. Their son's a deserter and a coward. You're not meant to kill your own.'

Lieutenant Hopwood felt he should try to uncover the original order given by Captain Wilson just to be absolutely certain the two young soldiers were guilty. Quite often in battle, orders are given verbally only but when a situation arises where a high risk factor is involved, the orders are recorded. He sent a telegram to the unit Head Quarters where Captain Wilson had been posted, requesting they do a search.

The Corporal who was assigned the task was a most diligent individual and began searching immediately. After a couple of hours he had not been successful and was about to give up when he found it. He quickly returned to his immediate superior, Captain Oats, and reported his find.

'Well you better call Poperinge straight away. Those soldiers are due to be shot at dawn.'

The Corporal headed for the communications hut to make the vital call.

'I need to make an urgent telephone call to Poperinge, Sergeant.'

'I am afraid you can't, sir.'

'What in hell do you mean?'

'The Germans knocked it out this morning. The only way we can try to get a message through is by pigeon.'

'If that's all we've got, that's what we'll use.'

The Corporal wrote the message and the Sergeant attached it to his best bird.

In Poperinge, the two condemned soldiers were in their cell hoping the sun wouldn't rise. Of course they knew that thought was futile. The time was four in the morning; sunrise was due at six o'clock.

'Percy, it's been a pleasure knowing you, mate.'

'You too, Tom. Are you scared?'

'I am fucking scared all right, mate. I didn't think it would end like this; here we are about to die and for what? We know we're innocent but these bastards want to kill us anyway. Why?'

At 5.30am, two guards entered the cell. They wrapped white cloth around their bodies and shackled their ankles. One of the guards placed a white patch over their hearts to give the shooters something to aim for.

The time was 5.50am.

Percy and Tom were carried to the courtyard where two-execution posts were located against a high brick wall. They were tied to the post and waited.

The messenger pigeon was only half a kilometre from the town and making good headway. It landed at 5.55am. Lieutenant Hopwood read the message; he ran the five hundred metres to the town hall where the executions were about to take place.

He entered the courtyard just as the firing squad fired their lethal volley. Both men slumped.

British Justice had been done.

On Flanders Fields
The Red Poppies Blow

Chapter 27

In Flanders fields the poppies blow
Between the crosses, row on row,
That mark our place; and in the sky
The larks, still bravely singing, fly
Scarce heard amid the guns below.

We are the Dead. Short days ago
We lived, felt dawn, saw sunset glow,
Loved, and were loved, and now we lie
In Flanders fields.

Take up our quarrel with the foe:
To you from failing hands we throw
The torch, be yours to hold it high.
If ye break faith with us who die
We shall not sleep, though poppies grow

In Flanders Fields
Lieutenant John McCrae

John McCrae was born in Ontario on November 30, 1872 into a military family. His father, David, was a Lieutenant Colonel in the Canadian Army. He and his wife, Janet, had two other children a daughter, Geills and a son, Tom.

The family was deeply religious being Scottish Presbyterians; both parents passed onto their children strong spiritual beliefs and compassion for both people and animals.

While he was a student, John began writing poetry; his works were regarded highly. John also showed a strong interest in the military, joining the Highfield Cadet Corps at age fourteen and at seventeen, he joined the Militia field battery; his father was the Commander.

John went on to graduate from Guelph Collegiate and won a scholarship to the University of Toronto. He attended for three years but was forced to take a year off due to severe asthma, a condition that recurred throughout his life

During that year he met a young woman, the sister of a good friend. John was besotted by the eighteen-year-old beauty but was devastated when she died. This experience was reflected in his poetry.

He returned to his studies in Toronto in 1893 and graduated with a Bachelor of Arts degree in 1894. He then attended the University of Toronto medical school.

John spent the summer of his third year as resident physician at the Garrett Hospital in Mount Airy outside Baltimore, a summer convalescent home for sick children. He wrote an essay about his young patients and frequently described the children in his correspondence.

A kitten has taken up with a poor (child) dying of muscular atrophy who cannot move. It stays with him all the time, and sleeps most of the day in his straw hat.

Tonight I saw the kitten curled up under the bedclothes. It seems as it were a gift of Providence that the little creature should attach itself to the child who needs it most. (Prescott, In Flanders Fields: The Story of John McCrae, p. 18)

While training as a doctor, he was also perfecting his skills as a poet. At university, he had sixteen poems and several short stories published in a variety of magazines, including 'Saturday Night'.

He also continued his connection with the military, becoming a gunner with the Number 2 Battery in Guelph in 1890, Quarter-Master Sergeant in 1891, Second Lieutenant in 1893 and Lieutenant in 1896. At university, he was a member of the Queen's Own Rifles of Canada, of which he became company captain.

In 1898, John McCrae received a Bachelor of Medicine degree and the gold medal from the University of Toronto medical school. He worked as resident house officer at Toronto General Hospital from 1898 to 1899.

In 1899, he went to Baltimore and interned at the Johns Hopkins Hospital where his brother Thomas had worked as assistant resident since 1895. There, both John and Thomas McCrae became close associates of Dr. William Osler, the pre-eminent medical educator of his time.

August 1914

The United Kingdom declared war on Germany, which triggered the start of World War I. Canada, as a Dominion within the British Empire, declared war also.

McCrae was appointed as a field surgeon in the Canadian artillery and was in charge of a field hospital during the Second Battle of Ypres in 1915. John's good friend, Lt. Alexis Helmer, was killed in the battle.

John was devastated, he had witnessed untold deaths since he arrived in Ypres; he had witnessed and treated horrendous injuries by both shrapnel and gas. He had amputated young soldiers' legs and arms and sown their faces back together but nothing could prepare him for losing such a good friend. After being given the news, he walked outside of the dressing station and sat down on the back of an ambulance next to the cemetery where Alexis would be buried and wrote "In Flanders Fields".

The iconic poem was first published in the magazine Punch in 1915.

The verses swiftly became one of the most popular poems of the war, used in countless fund-raising campaigns and frequently translated (a Latin version begins "In agro belgico..." "In Flanders Fields" was also extensively printed in the United States prior to them joining the war.

On January 28, 1918, while still commanding No. 3 Canadian General Hospital, McCrae died of pneumonia with "extensive pneumococcus meningitis". He was buried the following day in the Commonwealth War Graves Commission section of Wimereux Cemetery with full military honours. His flag-draped coffin was borne on a gun carriage and McCrae's charger, "Bonfire", preceded the mourners –who included Sir Arthur Currie, the Canadian General, and many of McCrae's friends and staff – with McCrae's boots reversed in the stirrups.

His famous words live on.

I'd Rather Play Footy

Chapter 28

Melbourne, Australia 1914

The day was a typical Melbourne winter's day, raining and cold with a westerly blowing. Jack Williams and his best mate George Hardwick were getting changed in the Bentleigh Football Ground's spartan change rooms to go out and do battle with their arch foe, Northcote. The two footballers had been playing together since primary school days at Bentleigh West. Jack and George lived in the same street and with some other kids from the neighbourhood often played kick to kick in the street.

Now they were both seventeen and were regarded as excellent footballers; Jack played at full forward and George played in the ruck. Both positions were regarded as critical to the team's overall performance.

The team ran onto the field to the applause of about twenty spectators, mostly relatives of the players; the second division didn't have a great following unlike the VFL, which attracted crowds of fifty thousand or more. A Collingwood / Carlton game had been known to pull in eighty thousand.

The two teams took their respective field positions; Northcote was favoured to win this contest.

The umpire blew his whistle and bounced the ball in the centre; it was on for young and old. By the final siren, the scores were Northcote 165 points, Bentleigh 86.

The mood in Bentleigh's change rooms was morose while the visitors were singing their team song and generally whooping it up.

Bentleigh's coach was a former VFL player, Charlie Daniel; he was not pleased with the team's performance. He approached Jack and George who were sitting on the bench together as they normally did.

> 'What in the fuck were you blokes playing out there? It wasn't fucking football. Both you blokes were "missing in action". You'd better lift your game or you won't get a run next week.'

They felt bad enough without the coach giving them a serve in front of the other players.

Jack and George showered in silence, dressed and went home.

The next week they played Sandringham and killed them; Bentleigh 186 Sandringham 92. They felt much better after that win; both Jack and George were named as best on ground.

June 28 1914

'Hey, Jack, what's all the fuss about with that Prince and his Mrs. getting shot over in Europe somewhere? I mean, what's it got to do with us?

'Fucked if I know, George, but they're certainly kicking up a fuss. It'll all die down eventually and then we call all get on with our lives. Just because bloody Austria is getting all upset, doesn't mean Britain will join the bloody fight.'

The European situation got progressively worse and the world watched and waited.

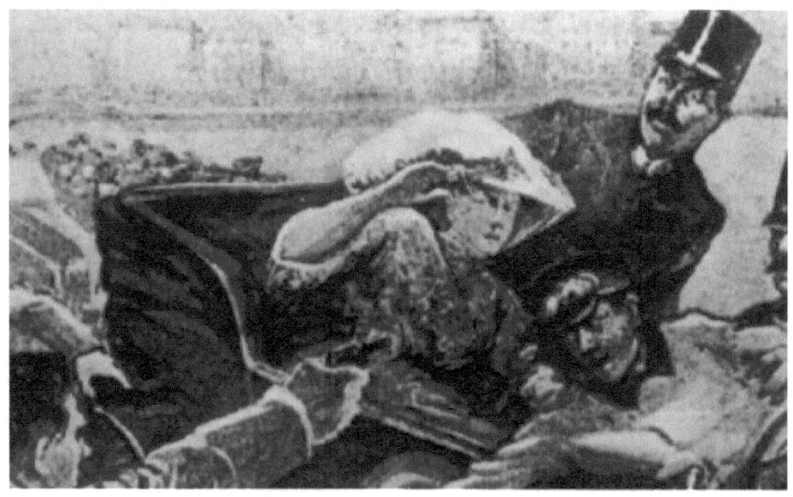

Assassination of Archduke Franz Ferdinand

Then.

EXTRA! THE ONION **EXTRA!**

WAR DECLARED BY ALL

AUSTRIA DECLARES WAR ON SERBIA DECLARES WAR ON GERMANY DECLARES WAR ON FRANCE DECLARES WAR ON TURKEY DECLARES WAR ON RUSSIA DECLARES WAR ON BULGARIA DECLARES WAR ON BRITAIN

OTTOMAN EMPIRE ALMOST DECLARES WAR ON ITSELF

NATIONS STRUGGLE TO REMEMBER ALLIES

AREA DRUNKARD DECLARES WAR ON IRELAND

Jack called around to George's house; they walked out to the spacious back yard with its fruit trees and rose bushes.

'What do ya reckon we should do, cobber?'

'About what?'

'You know what I bloody mean; are we going to enlist?'

'I dunno, mate; I think so. It could be a bit dangerous but yet again we'll see a bit of the world. They reckon the war will be over by Christmas so we get to go on the grand tour for nix.'

'Yeah I think you're right. Let's do it.'

Both boys had just turned eighteen so they didn't need parental approval. They decided to go into town the next day and turn up at Victoria Barracks to sign up.

They arrived the next morning only to find a line that stretched five hundred metres down St Kilda Road.

They took two hours to reach the enlistment office where a tall burly Sergeant greeted them. He was very friendly and accommodating and helped them completed the appropriate forms.

The next step was the physical examination. Both Jack and George passed with flying colours. They were accepted and were assigned into the fifth Battalion. Their adventure of a lifetime had begun! They were allocated their uniforms and had their photograph taken.

Best Mates

Let the Adventure Begin

Chapter 29

The two proud Diggers returned home on the train with the other passengers congratulating them and wishing them well. They walked the two miles from the station laughing and imagining what might lie before them.

'I hope these fucking boots become more comfortable, Jack, my feet are killing me.'

'Don't worry mate with all the marching they're gunna make us do, they'll soon wear in.'

'Yeah I suppose ya right.'

They reached McKittrick Street and paused.

'How ya going to break it to ya Mum and Dad, Jack?'

' Well, walking in wearing this uniform might give 'em a pretty good hint!'

'Yeah, I suppose it will.'

'Are you a bit worried, mate?'

'Dad was in the Boer War; he never talks about it but I reckon it was pretty rough. I reckon he's gunna be a bit worried. Mum will just cry.'

She'll be right, George; once they get over the initial shock, they'll be waving the flag as we march off.'

Jack was right; after both their parents were reconciled to the fact that their sons were going off to war, they became very supportive.

Both Jack and George had younger brothers: Tim was Jack's brother and Richard was George's. The age difference was two years.

When the younger brothers learnt of their brothers' enlistment, they were envious.

'It's not fair. You're going off overseas and we're stuck here,' complained Tim.

'Yeah, just you wait. When we're older enough, we're coming over and we can all fight together,' added Richard.

'I wouldn't hold my breath, mate. I think the war would be long over by the time you turn eighteen,' George commiserated.

Two weeks after enlisting, the two young Diggers were transported to Broadmeadows, a make-shift training camp, where they were trained to use bayonets, rifles and entrenching tools.

The camp became a quagmire; it was difficult to get around and many of the new recruits came down with dysentery. Not a great start to Army life.

After two months, they boarded a ship at Princes Pier bound for Albany in Western Australia.

They made that trip without incident, berthing in Albany and departing two days later, bound for Egypt, a place they had only read about.

1915 Egypt

Jack and George and hundreds of other new recruits boarded the troop ship, *SS Ceramic*, the largest troop ship in the fleet. It had been used as a cruise liner but all the luxurious trappings had been removed. This was no bloody cruise. After two months of rough weather and high seas and countless games of "two up", they disembarked at a place Jack and George had never heard of before: Serapeum, Alexandria, Egypt. Both boys had always wanted to see the pyramids and were disappointed there were none to be seen. There were, however, lots of ancient ruins to climb but it was bloody hot and the hawkers would not leave them alone.

After about a week of heat and sand storms they were moved to a new camp at Mena, near Cairo. Now Jack and George could see the pyramids and the sphinx, something they were all looking forward to when they had been on the "cruise".

SS Ceramic 1915

The two young adventurers became tourists climbing the Great Pyramid and taking camel rides. There were other benefits also: they could go into Cairo, a city like they had never seen before. The boys had only seen Melbourne, so Cairo with its exotic people and nightlife was something to behold. They were pretty well-behaved, although on one occasion they ran foul of the military police.

They had been drinking in a Cairo bar and didn't realise the time. Two British MPs entered the premises and declared that all the soldiers were in breach of the twelve o'clock curfew. They required each soldier to give his name and number and assured the twenty odd Australians that charges would be laid.

The Aussies all bolted at once, knocking over one of the MPs and running through the still crowded laneways. None of them, including George and Jack, was caught. They sneaked back into the camp and slept like babies.

Post Card From Egypt

Digger Tourists

Gallipoli

Where the Hell is Gallipoli?

Chapter 30

The Australian troops did a bit more than play tourists during their Egyptian posting; they were ordered to march with full packs from Cairo to the Suez Canal in forty degree heat across the desert. Many dropped from heat exhaustion; the remainder arrived completely spent. McCay, the Australian General, had ordered the march to toughen up the Diggers before they were shipped off to fight. He was widely criticised for this ludicrous exercise.

Orders had been received by High Command to ship the Australian and New Zealand troops (ANZACs) to invade Turkey, landing at a place called Gallipoli. British troops were also involved.

Winston Churchill proposed to break through the Dardanelles - the narrow sea passage from the Mediterranean leading towards the Ottoman capital, Istanbul, and the Black Sea. His plan was not accepted by the whole of cabinet and the military but after seven weeks of rancorous debate, he prevailed.

George and Jack were at last going to see some action; they were both excited and nervous about the prospect of fighting the Turks. Neither of them had even heard of Turkey before, let alone Gallipoli.

They were herded onto a ship called the *HMAS Armadale* along with a thousand other men. They were amused by the ship's name; "Armadale" was a suburb of Melbourne and it was one of the football teams they played against in their competition.

24th April 1915

A flotilla of troop ships, escorted by warships, sailed off to Gallipoli; the next day, the 25^{th,} would be the day they landed; a day that would go down in the annals of history.

'Hey, Jack, this is the best tucker we've had since we joined the fucking army.'

'Yeah it's bloody good. I hope it's not like the last meal they give somebody before they hang the poor bastard.'

'Yeah, I know what you mean, mate. Anyway let's get stuck in.

It may be the last fucking meal we ever eat.'

The young ANZACs rested as much as they could, but it was difficult when the bloke next door was snoring and farting and there was nowhere to move.

About two in the morning, the officers moved around amongst the men, waking those who were sleeping and giving words of encouragement to those already awake.

The instruction was that they were to climb down rope ladders into the boats. These boats would be towed close to shore and then they would be rowed the rest of the way.

25th April 1915, 3.30 am

The time to go had arrived.

Jack and George, the Bentleigh boys, slowly lowered themselves down into the landing craft, which was rocking quite severely.

'Right, mate, we're on our way to fame and glory.'

'I don't know about that, George.'

'Just kidding, mate. How are ya feeling?'

'Yeah, okay, George. You make sure you stick by me, mate, we've got to protect each other's arses, right?'

'You bet, Jack, no worries.'

As the boats were towed towards the shore, there were only muted whispers among the soldiers. After about forty very long minutes, they were cast off to make the remainder of the journey on their own, under oar.

There was an eerie silence as the landing boats slipped through the sea; the only sound was the water lapping the sides of the craft.

They heard a shot and then another.

'Shit, they've spotted us. Can't be too many of the buggers if that's all they can throw at us!' exclaimed the officer in charge of the craft.

With that, a cacophony of gun and cannon exploded around them. Bullets were hitting the boats and the water. They also were hitting the young inexperienced soldiers from a faraway land.

'Keep ya fucking head down, Jack.'

'Don't you worry, mate, I bloody well am.'

Jack felt a warm slimy substance running down his face.

'Shit! I think I've been hit.'

'No you haven't, it's the bloke next to ya's brain.'

'Holy fuck, the poor bastard!'

Jack wiped the grey substance from his face with his army-issued handkerchief. They were getting close to the beach; bodies were floating everywhere and the Turks were blasting them from all sides. The water had turned red.

'Right men, out you get and give them hell!' shouted the officer.

He used a leather megaphone so he could be heard over the battle noise.

'Remember we've got to stick together, mate!' Jack yelled in a quivering voice.

'You bet, Jack.'

They both jumped out, one after the other and sank down into the chest-high water. They found it difficult wading through to the beach with their heavy packs while holding their 303 Enfield rifles above their heads but they both made it: many didn't.

First Troops Land

The two Diggers ran for the craggy cliffs, hoping to get some cover from the relentless onslaught. They lay against the cliff face and looked up but they couldn't see a bloody Turk, just the sound of their machine guns and shells.

Their commanding officer, Lieutenant Westgarth, crawled up to them.

'Lads, we need to start making our way up the cliffs and establish some sort of camp.'

Jack and George looked up again.

'How the fuck are we supposed to get up there? Abdul has got us covered; as soon as we stick our necks out, the bastards are gunna blow our heads off,' whispered George.

'Okay, let's get up there and give Johnny Turk some of his own, boys.'

They had no other choice; the platoon started up the sandy cliff, the rocks crumbled from under their feet making progress difficult. The Turkish onslaught continued unabated and several Aussie Diggers fell. They reached a plateau and it was here where they would remain for the next twenty-four hours.

A shallow trench was dug giving them some protection but not much.

Eventually the Turks started to pull back from the ridges under heavy allied shelling. This allowed the Australians to progress to a more secure line and dig more substantial trenches. For the next eight months they fought the Turks with many thousands from both sides dying.

August 6 1915

One of the most significant and famous assaults of the Gallipoli campaign, the Battle of Lone Pine, was intended as a diversion from attempts by the New Zealand and Australian units to force a breakout from the ANZAC perimeter on the heights of Chanuk Bair and Hill 971.

The ANZACs shelled the overcrowded Turkish trenches for some hours before the charge. The ANZAC forces, consisting of 1st, 2nd, 3rd, 4th Battalions, entered the main Turkish trenches within half an hour. The 5th, 6th, 7th, 8th and 12th Battalions reinforced the First Brigade the next day. The battle raged for four days.

The Turks had established a labyrinth of log-covered trenches and it was in this environment the two sides fought. There was total confusion and amid screams of anguish and despair, Lone Pine became a furious nightmare of hand-to-hand combat.

'We were like a mob of ferrets in a rabbit warren' one ANZAC said. ' It was one long grave, only some of us were still alive in it'.

Hundreds of ferocious one-on-one struggles broke out in the maze of trenches. Turks killed Turks and ANZACs killed ANZACs in the confusion. Both sides hurled bombs at each other, which were lobbed back and forth until they exploded. The Turkish trenches were floored with the bodies of the dead and wounded of both sides.

Both Jack and George were in the 5th Battalion; they waited in the trenches as the battle raged on during the first day of Lone Pine. They could hear the screaming and the sounds of death but could do nothing. Their turn came on the second day.

Trench at Lone Pine

August 7^{th,} 1915

'Right, men, we are going to join our comrades and relieve them from what seemed like a bloody tough fight. They've done the hard work; now we should be able to go in and mop up, as it were,' Lieutenant Westgarth stated.

'Okay, this where it really gets tough. What we've experienced up until now has been a teddy bears' picnic.'

'Yeah, mate; you scared?

'Fucking oath, mate, of cause I'm scared but I reckon we'll show Abdul a thing or two about fighting.'

'Bloody Oath!' responded George.

Lieutenant Westgarth blew his whistle; they all clambered over the top and ran towards the Turkish line. The first day's battalions had been successful in capturing the Turkish trenches so it was just a hundred yard sprint. There were no machine guns to greet them but the Turks were heavily shelling no-man's land. Many fell.

For the next three days, the Turks, intent on retrieving their lost line, blasted them with heavy artillery.

At the cessation of The Battle of Loan Pine, the ANZACs sustained two thousand two hundred and seventy three casualties. The Turks lost between five and seven thousand.

George and Jack survived the ordeal and went on to fight other battles around the Gallipoli Peninsula.

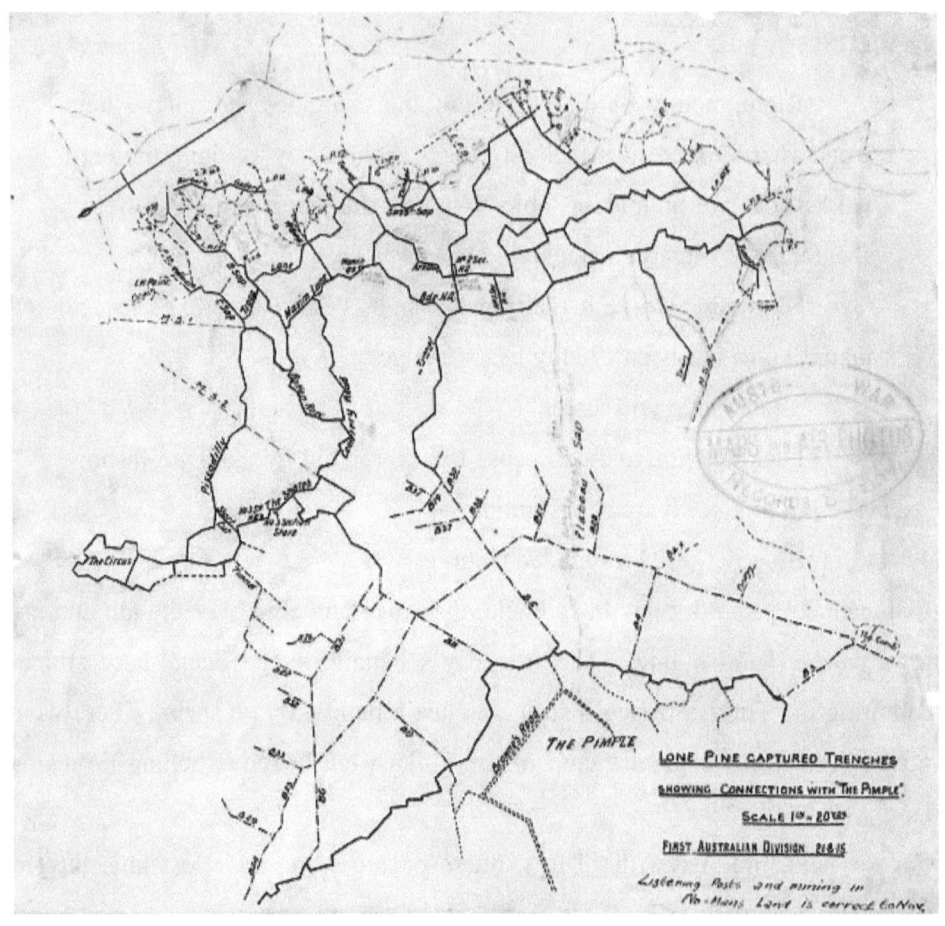

LONE PINE CAPTURED TRENCHES
SHOWING CONNECTIONS WITH THE PIMPLE.
SCALE 1in = 20yds
FIRST AUSTRALIAN DIVISION 21.8.15

Christmas was approaching and the weather was getting very cold.

'Jack, do you think we are ever going to leave this god-forsaken place, mate?'

'Fuck, I hope so, George. I don't want to end my days here; I'm looking forward to dying when I'm eighty something and the grand kiddies will be standing around my bed waiting for me to go.'

'Yeah, me too.'

An officer heard the conversation and approached the two Diggers.'

'I don't think you need to worry too much fellas, you may be out
of here sooner than you think.'

He was right.

On January 8, 1916, Allied forces staged a full retreat from the shores of the Gallipoli Peninsula, ending a disastrous invasion of the Ottoman Empire. The Gallipoli Campaign resulted in two hundred and fifty thousand Allied casualties and greatly discredited Allied military command. Roughly three hundred thousand Turks were killed or wounded.

The Gallipoli campaign was only the beginning; George and Jack were to experience more bloody battles. They sailed off to France to join their comrades on the Western Front.

Both Jack and George felt it was an appropriate time to write to their younger brothers back home in Melbourne. They had written letters to their Mums and Dads but as the young lads were approaching enlistment age, they thought a letter to try to deter them would be the right thing to do.

You Wouldn't Want to be Here
Chapter 31

The troop ships taking the Gallipoli survivors formed a large convoy steaming towards Marseilles, France. This gave the Diggers some free time to write home.

January 7, 1916

Dear Tim,

I'm sorry I haven't written sooner but I've been a bit busy of late. George and me are both well considering where we've been and what we've been doing. Right now we're on a ship heading for France. I believe we're going up north to the Western Front to fight the bloody Germans. It'll make a nice change from fighting the Turks.

You would have read about Gallipoli in the papers but no paper could describe what the place was like. George and me were together in the same mob so that was good but the conditions were bloody horrible. The trenches were either boiling hot and steamy or freezing cold and snowing. Neither of us had ever seen snow before and I can tell you we bloody don't want to see the stuff again. When it melts it makes the trenches and no man's land a muddy quagmire. When we weren't fighting the Turks we just sat around being bored. We had to cook our own food, which wasn't too bad, but as time wore on the rations got leaner and leaner. Bully beef jam and stale bread and tea was the order of the day. The flies could carry a man away and the rats were as big as cats.

The fighting was pretty bad, the Turks are good fighters I'll give them that. Mind you they shriek like girls when they feel the cold steel of a bayonet.

I'd never seen a dead person before I came here now, I see hundreds everyday both our blokes and theirs. I reckon it's got to make you hard.

So the grand adventure we signed up for has been hell and it isn't gunna get any better.

Stay at home Tim it's not worth it look after Mum and Dad for me.

I don't know when I'll be home but hopefully this war will end soon.

Love

Your Big Brother

Jack

Jack posted the letter to his brother on January 10; Tim didn't receive it until March 31st , two weeks after he and his good mate, Dick, had enlisted. Now there would be four brothers from McKittrick Street fighting on the Western Front.

After eight weeks' training at Broadmeadows, Tim and Dick sailed off for the great adventure.

Brothers in Arms

Chapter 32

Dick and Tim took the same route as their big brothers, sailing from Victoria Dock, Melbourne for Albany, Western Australia. They then endured a six-week trip to Marseilles, France. The train trip to St Omer was enjoyable in that they saw some beautiful countryside. The two young soldiers, along with the rest of their battalion, marched thirty miles to Armentieres. The two lads were lucky they had been billeted in the same barn.

'Are you asleep yet, Dick?'

'How in the hell do you think I can sleep, Tim? Those cannon are shaking the whole building. The Sergeant told me we're about ten miles from the front; if you think it's loud here, what could it be like at the front?'

'Well, mate, we find out tomorrow.'

'I wonder where Jack and George are now? Wouldn't it be great if we ran into them?'

'Yeah, it would.'

'Well I'm gunna try and get some sleep, it'll be a big day tomorrow. Goodnight, Dick.'

'Goodnight, mate.'

19th July 1915 Fromelles

Jack Williams and George Hardwick were waiting in their recently dug trench; they were well aware there was a formidable enemy waiting for them across no man's land.

This would be no easy task as the width of no man's land was about four hundred metres and the Germans had been entrenched in their well- built fortifications for nearly two years. The Fifth Division had dug their trenches in the last ten days, hardly a match for Jerry.

Their heavy artillery had been bombarding the German line for the past seven hours and they both knew the time to go over the top was close at hand.

> 'Jack, who are we, mate?'

> 'I dunno. Who are we?'

> 'We're the Bentleigh boys.'

> *'Razza, Razza, Razza, whiskers on your dazza.*

> *Who, who, who are we?*

> *We are the boys from Bentleigh*

> *Let's kill em boys.'*

They both laughed but didn't lose the true meaning of the team chant.

> 'Hey, George, what's that noise?'

> 'What noise, mate?'

> 'Exactly. There's no fucking noise. The bombardment is over.'

Both knew that meant only one thing; over the top.

The three-minute whistle blew; both of them checked their bayonets and grenades. The final whistle sounded and their officer, Lieutenant Duffy, called out.

> 'Right, boys, go give them hell.'

Jack was third in line, George was fourth. Jack looked down on George from the ladder.

      'Don't forget, mate, we're Bentleigh boys.'

      'Razza Razza Razza,' came the reply.

They both reached solid ground and started to run across the pock- marked landscape.

The noise was deafening; machine gun fire plus rifle fire and grenades made it impossible to communicate. Every man was on his own, or so it felt.

The 59th had been ordered to take "Sugar Loaf", the major Kraut gun emplacement, which was mowing down the Diggers like sheaves of corn.

The two Diggers had made it about half way to their objective; there were bodies of soldiers everywhere. Some had been blown apart by German shells, others had been ripped apart by the lethal German machine guns. The rats were scurrying amongst the dead; it was a banquet for them.

      'Mate, we've got no fucking choice; we can't go back. The only thing we can do is go forward,' yelled Jack.

      'You're right, mate, if we're going to die in this God-forsaken paddock, let's go out in a blaze of glory and take that concrete shithouse out.'

Jack and Jim almost made it to the base of the gun emplacement when a German machine gun ripped them both apart.

Razza, Razza, Razza.

I Just Want to be Like My Big Brother

Chapter 33

Tim and Dick were woken by their Sergeant at 6 am. They assembled in the mess tent where they were served a hearty breakfast before being trucked off to a little village called Fromelles.

July 17, 1916

Unbeknown to the two friends, their elder brothers were further down the battle line.

Jack Williams and George Hardwick were in the 15th Brigade, 59th Battalion, directly in front of "Sugar Loaf".

Their younger brothers, Tim Williams and Dick Hardwick were in the 8th Brigade, 29th Battalion, at the far end of the line.

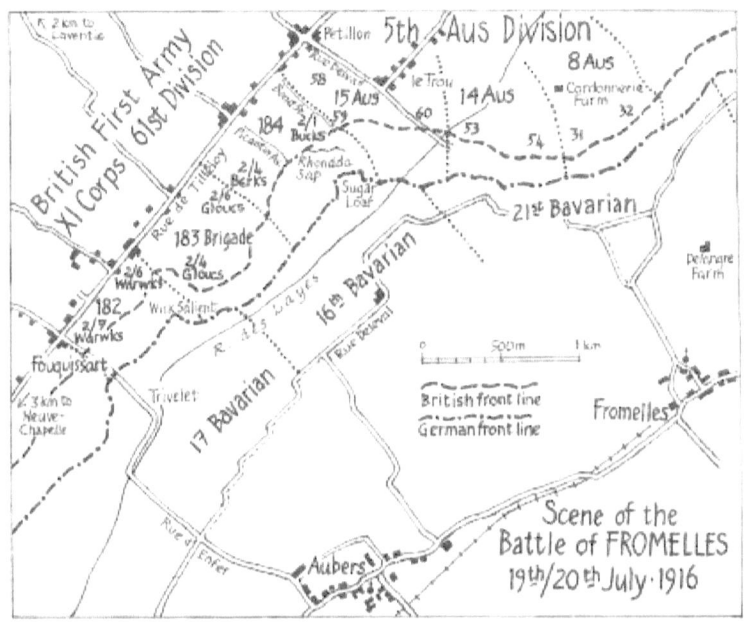

Scene of the Battle of FROMELLES 19th/20th July·1916

The two novice soldiers had seen no action to date so they were looking forward to giving the Germans some real stick.

While waiting for the signal to go over the top, Dick decided he would write a note to his Mum and Dad.

Dear Mum and Dad,

I am just about to enter my first battle. We've been bombing the hell out of the German positions for many hours and my commander tells us they will probably be already dead by the time we go over the top. I hope not, because I want to shoot a few. (Sorry, Mum).

I know Jack and George are on the front somewhere but I wouldn't have a clue where. Tim and me hope we will run into them soon.

There goes the three-minute whistle so I better go. I'll whack this letter in my top pocket just in case the worst happens.

All my love

Your Son, Dick

The tension in the trench was intense; they knew the distance to the German lines was about four hundred metres. That would be a perilous crossing if the officers were wrong and Fritz was waiting for them. No man's land was now littered with shell holes so it was not going to be a walk in the park.

Their commander, a young Lieutenant named Shearer, was moving through the trench giving all the boys encouragement and making sure bayonets were fixed.

He opened his fob watch and checked the time; he blew the whistle.

The Aussie Diggers climbed the ladders and commenced their assault across that God- forsaken strip of land called no man's land.

Tim was first over the top with Dick a little way back. They were running, ducking and weaving, trying to avoid the bodies of their mates strewn across the muddy earth.

Tim was on his belly, firing at the enemy when a shell landed directly on his back. There was nothing left to identify him after the battle.

Dick knew nothing of his good friend's demise; he was concentrating on getting to the German trenches. He made it. Jumping over the parapet, he shot one enemy soldier and bayoneted another. He moved down the trench and found a large dug-out. He entered cautiously and could not see anything; obviously the officers had nicked off. Not all of them; a German Captain standing in the shadows shot Dick twice in the forehead so he was dead before hitting the ground.

Dick and Tim, like their big brothers, were corpses, killed in battle.

I Just Want to be with my Boys
Chapter 34

Melbourne July 1916

Roy Wilson had been a postman for the best part of twenty years; he enjoyed the job, particularly when the weather was fine. People looked out for Roy riding his red P.M.G bicycle along their street hoping they would receive a letter or a birthday card.

Since the war had begun and Australia started sending troops to fight in Turkey, France and the Middle East, his job had become less enjoyable. He felt like he was the "Grim Reaper" delivering messages of death and despair.

If he was required to deliver the dreaded yellow telegram, he had to hand it over personally; he couldn't just place it in the letterbox.

He had seen too many faces of parents who had opened the front door to see him standing there. They didn't need to open the envelope: they knew what it said; 'It is with deep regret...' The anguish and despair of those poor people; he would never get used to it.

It was a cold and rainy morning on the thirtieth of July; Roy was hoping there would be no one home at number eight and number ten McKittrick Street. He cycled up to number eight, rested his red bicycle against the gate and walked slowly up to the front door. He hesitated and then rang the bell; there was no immediate response so for a moment he thought there was no one home. However, the door opened. It was Mrs Hardwick. She looked at Roy and screamed as she ran down the hall, calling for her husband, Frank. Frank Hardwick appeared a few minutes later.

'What is it, Roy?'

'I'm sorry, Frank, truly sorry, mate.'

Roy handed over the two envelopes.

Frank looked at Roy in dismay.

'Two! You've given me two. There must be a mistake… nobody gets two!'

'I'm so sorry, Frank, if there is anything I can do…'

'I think you've fucking done enough already.'

Frank closed the door in Roy's face. Roy returned to his bike, not to ride but to retrieve another two yellow envelopes.

He had the same experience with William and Emma Williams next door.

When Roy had finished his round, he went straight home and drank a couple of whiskies in front of the fire. The whisky tasted good but could not ease his sadness.

Frank and Sophie Hardwick tried to cope with the knowledge that both their sons, George and Richard (Dick), had been taken from them but it was proving very difficult. Sophie would cry at the slightest provocation, where Frank became very quiet and reflective. His mood swings grew progressively worse over the ensuing months. His mates at work in the Victorian railways were very concerned. They knew how much he loved his sons but could not understand his almost reclusive behaviour. He shunned all his friends, always ate alone and had no conversation with anybody.

On the 23rd of December, 1916, Frank went out to his backyard shed, where he spent a lot of time making bits and pieces out of wood and steel.

He took a thick rope and threw it over a roof beam, and climbing onto a chair, he placed a noose around his neck and kicked the chair away.

That is how his wife Sophie found him when she went out to the shed to call him for his dinner as six o'clock.

He had left a note for her.

I just want to be with my Boys

Death of the Innocents
Chapter 35

Aerschot is a simple town in an area known as Flemish Brabant. It has no grand buildings or picturesque town squares. The only people seen in the village were its inhabitants- no tourists. The townspeople went about their business without fuss. Saturdays were the exception; the town square would come alive when the farmers' market was held.

The only other sign of life was Sunday when mass was held in the village church. Flemish life tended to be simple and traditional, a very peaceful way of living.

The surrounding farmers grew corn and wheat and raised cattle and sheep; they were the economic lifeblood of Aerschot.

The war had had no real effect on the village or its lifestyle until:19 August 1914

At nine o'clock in the morning, German troops came marching into the town square.

The Burgomaster (Chief Magistrate) had a fifteen-year-old son, who raced to his father's house to close the Venetian shutters. Some of the soldiers were firing their weapons and shot the young lad in the leg.

Soon after the incident, the Burgomaster, Mr Tielemans was summoned to the Town Hall by the commanding officer.

'Your son tried to shoot one of my men, you filthy schweinhund'

(pig dog; a species indigenous to Germany)

'I assure you, sir, he didn't, he doesn't even own a weapon.'

'Don't you dare argue with me, you piece of filth. Come here.'

Tielemans approached the officer with great trepidation.

The officer smashed his revolver against the Burgomaster's face causing significant bleeding.

'I am occupying your pathetic filthy house as my head quarters; now go.'

Colonel Stenger and his two aides-de-camp went directly to the house where they ransacked the bedrooms. They then stepped out onto the balcony and watched the march-past of their troops.

Some idiotic soldiers started to fire around the square and a bullet hit the colonel. One of the aides-de-camp rushed down into the square shouting:

'The colonel has been murdered. Bring me the Burgomaster.'

'I think they are going to kill me, my darling.'

'Be courageous, my love.'

Two German soldiers grabbed him, marching him off to the Town Hall to be interrogated.

'Please spare him; he does not own a weapon and neither does my son,' pleaded his wife.

The German soldier just sneered at her.

'Who cares? We know he did it. Where's your pimply son? We want him too.'

They found the boy and dragged him off to join his father, kicking him the whole way.

'Come with me, you whore, back to your cess- pit of a house. I want to make sure you're not hiding anybody.'

He dragged Madame Tielemans by the hair back to the house and with his service revolver pointed at her the whole time, checked every room. When they arrived back in the kitchen, her daughter, Françoise was waiting for them.

'What are you going to do with us?' protested Françoise.

'You will be shot, along with your mother and your servants,' came his cold reply.

The Germans began their methodical pillaging of the village, setting fire to all the houses. Any protesters were shot.

Madame Tielemans watched as soldiers left her house with armfuls of wine while the contents of the rooms were also removed

She left the house, not wanting to witness the destruction of what once was her life.

Looking through the smoke haze and lurid light of the fires, she spotted her husband and son along with her brother-in-law being led to execution. She saw his face ashen and forlorn and her son with terror in his eyes.

'What should I do? Should I call out and tell them I love them?

No, it would not help things.'

The Germans herded the entire population of women and the condemned men out of town passing corpses along the way. They eventually reached their destination, a large field.

They pushed the women and girls into a cattle pen and that's where they slept.

The men had their hands tied behind their backs with thin copper wire so tight it drew blood. They were forced to lie face down and were forbidden to make any sound or move.

The women could see their village burning in the distance.

Just before dawn, the Germans decided it was time for the executions to commence.

The Burgomaster, his son and his brother were to be the first to be shot. They assembled about one hundred villagers to witness the execution.

'It is your time to die, Burgomaster,' an officer said.

'No, please, I will go in his place,' pleaded another citizen, Claes van Nuffel, 'The village needs him.'

'No, he must die.'

The Burgomaster was permitted to speak.

'I thank my good friend and political adversary for his kind and brave offer. I die knowing I have lived a good life and have tried to help others. I will not beg for mercy but I do beg for my son and brother's lives. Without me, my wife and daughter will need their support.'

The German officer just grinned and remained silent.

The young lad joined his father and uncle standing straight and looking directly at the firing squad.

The six German soldiers were ten yards from the three innocents; the officer lowered his sword and all three fell.

The Burgomaster's wife was heard to whisper with tears in her eyes: 'the best man in this world has ceased to exist.'

The Germans then lined all the men in groups of three; the third man was the one to be shot, they were required to step back three paces. Once there were about fifty men selected, the soldiers went along the line, killing each in turn. It was a horrific scene, with dead bodies all in a row and the terrified survivors standing their ground.

A few days after the massacre at Aerschot, on the 23rd of August, 1914, Dinant, another quiet village, became the scene of wholesale massacres which involved exactly six hundred and six victims, including eleven children under five years old, twenty-eight of ages between ten and fifteen and seventy-one women.

War is a horrible business and of the thirty five million casualties suffered in World War one, many millions were civilians. How many were massacred in cold blood?

Over Paid, Over Here and Over Sexed

The Americans are Coming

Chapter 36

1917 France

The United States President, Woodrow Wilson, was very reluctant to enter World War One. He declared U.S neutrality and insisted that both sides respect America's rights as a neutral country.

Americans were deeply divided about the war in Europe, and how involvement could disrupt progressive reforms. "Top of the Pops" at the time was "I Didn't Raise My Boy to be a Soldier".

In 1916, Wilson narrowly won re-election with a slogan "He kept us out of the war."

Although claiming neutrality, it became clear that America began to lean towards Britain and France.

Wilson knew that wartime trade with the belligerents was important to the American economy and trade had boomed with the Allies.

The cash reserves of the Allies and the Germans were being eaten up by the war effort; they asked the USA for a line of credit and so in October 1915, President Wilson approved loans to both sides, although the Allies were the biggest benefactors. Loans to the Allies totalled $2.25 billion by 1917; on the other hand, Germany had loans outstanding of $27 million.

Germany announced a resumption of unrestricted submarine warfare in January 1917, which was an extremely provocative move, particularly after Germany sank the "Lusitania" in 1915 killing almost 2,000 people, many of them Americans.

Germany was bullish about winning the war within five months and therefore, even if America entered the war, it could not mobilise quickly enough to change the course of the war, or so Germany thought.

What really pushed Wilson to the limit of his patience was the "Zimmerman Telegram", a telegram which said that if Mexico went to war with the United States, Germany promised to help Mexico recover the territory it had lost during the 1840s, including Texas, New Mexico, California, and Arizona.

That telegram and the fact that Germany attacked three US ships during March, led Wilson to ask Congress for a "declaration of war".

In 1917, a senior German official scoffed at American might:

"America from a military point-of-view means nothing, and again nothing, and for a third time nothing."

The U.S. Army at the time had only 107,641men. Within a year, however, the United States raised a five million-man army. By the war's end, the American armed forces were a decisive factor in blunting a German offensive and ending the bloody stalemate.

To raise troops, President Wilson insisted on a military draft. More than twenty three million men registered during World War I, and 2,800,000 draftees served in the armed forces. To select officers, the army launched an ambitious program of psychological testing.

In March 1918, the Germans launched a massive offensive on the Western Front in France's Somme River valley. With German troops barely fifty miles from Paris, Marshal Ferdinand Foch, the leader of the French army, assumed command of the allied forces. Foch's troops, aided by eighty five thousand American soldiers, launched a furious counter-offensive. By the end of October, the counter-attack pushed the German army back to the Belgian border.

American entry into the war quickly overcame the German military's numerical advantage. In June 1918, some two hundred and seventy nine thousand American soldiers crossed the Atlantic; in July, over three hundred thousand; in August, two hundred and eighty six thousand more. All told, one and a half million American troops arrived in Europe during the last six months of the war. By the end of the conflict, the allies could field six hundred thousand more men than the Germans, at any one time. American troops fought in many battles including: Third Battle of the Aisne; Battle of Ambos Nogales; Battle of Amiens (1918); Battle of Belleau Wood; Battle of Blanc Mont Ridge; Battle of Cambrai (1917); Battle of Cantigny; Battle of Château-Thierry (1918); Battle of Hamel; Advance to the Hindenburg Line; Hundred Days Offensive; Lost Battalion (World War I); Second Battle of the Marne; Battle of Matz; Meuse-Argonne Offensive; Operation Michael; Battle of the Mountain of Reims; Rouge Bouquet; Battle of St. Quentin Canal; Battle of Saint-Mihiel and Battle of Tardenois.

Who Let the Dog Out?

Chapter 37

One of the greatest American warriors to fight in World War One was Sergeant Stubby. He fought in many battles and was a fearless and skilled soldier.

Sergeant Stubby Displaying His Medals

While training for combat on the fields of Yale University in 1917, Private J. Robert Conroy found a brindle puppy with a short tail. He named him "Stubby", and soon the dog became the mascot of the 102nd Infantry, 26th Yankee Division. He learned the bugle calls, the drills, and even a modified dog salute as he put his right paw on his right eyebrow.

Stubby had a positive effect on morale, and was allowed to remain in the camp, even though animals were forbidden. When the division shipped out for France aboard the SS Minnesota, Private Conroy smuggled Stubby aboard. Stubby hid in the coal bin until the ship was far out to sea. The intrepid canine was brought out on deck to the amazement of the soldiers and sailors. Stubby soon won over the ship's company. He was once again smuggled off the ship and was soon discovered by Private Conroy's commanding officer. The officer allowed Stubby to remain after Stubby gave him a salute. When the Yankee Division headed for the front lines in France, Stubby was given special orders allowing him to accompany the Division to the front lines as their official mascot. The 102nd Infantry reached the front lines on 5th February 1918. Stubby soon became accustomed to the loud rifles and heavy artillery fire; he never flinched.

Gas, an insidious weapon that caused horrendous injury, was used by all sides in the conflict. Stubby was one of those injured by gas and he was taken to a nearby field hospital and nursed back to health. His experience left him sensitive to the tiniest trace of gas. When the Division was attacked in an early morning gas attack, most of the troops were asleep. Stubby recognized it was gas and ran through the trench barking and biting at the soldiers, rousing them to sound the gas alarm, saving many from injury.

Stubby also had a talent for locating wounded men caught in no man's land. He could decipher the difference between English and German; if it was an English-speaking soldier he would bark until paramedics arrived. If they did not arrive and the wounded could walk, he would lead the lost soldiers back to the safety of the trenches. He even caught a German soldier mapping out the layout of the Allied trenches. The soldier called to Stubby in German; Stubby put his ears back and began to bark. As the German ran, the dog- soldier bit him on the legs, causing the German to trip and fall. He continued to attack the man until one of

Stubby's comrades arrived. For capturing an enemy spy, Stubby was put in for a promotion to the rank of Sergeant by the commander of the 102nd Infantry. He became the first dog to be given rank in the United States Armed Forces.

On another occasion, Stubby was injured during a grenade attack, receiving a large amount of shrapnel in his chest and leg. He was rushed to a field hospital and later transferred to a Red Cross Recovery Hospital for additional surgery. When Stubby became well enough to move around at the hospital, he visited wounded soldiers, boosting their morale. By the end of the war, Stubby had served in seventeen battles. He led the American troops in a 'pass and review' parade and later visited with President Woodrow Wilson. He visited the White House twice and met Presidents Harding and Coolidge. Stubby was awarded many medals for his heroism, including a medal from the Humane Society, which was presented by General John Pershing, the Commanding General of the United States Armies. He was awarded a membership in the American Legion and the Y.M.C.A.

When his master, J. Robert Conroy, began studying law at Georgetown University, Stubby became the mascot of the Georgetown Hoyas. He died in 1926.

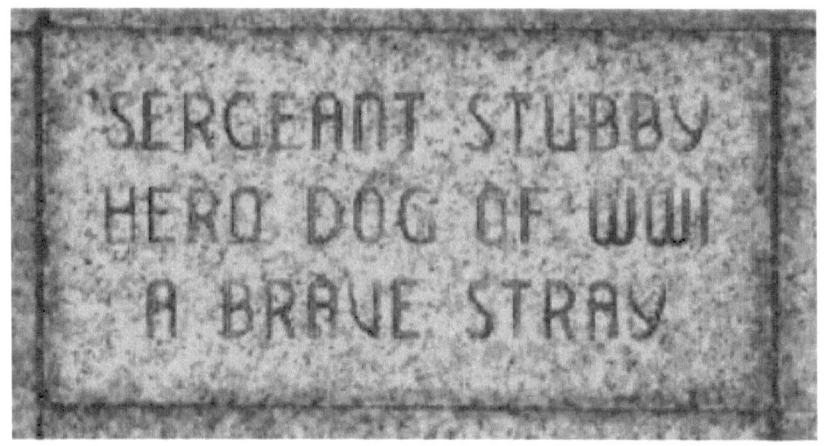

'World War One saw the first large scale use of war dogs in military history, and it was no longer more or less haphazard but organized and specialized.

During the Great War, vast numbers of dogs were employed as: sentries; messengers; ammunition carriers, pigeon carriers and food carriers; scouts; sled dogs; draught dogs; guard dogs; ambulance dogs; ratters; Red Cross casualty dogs and even cigarette dogs. It's estimated that Germany employed over 30,000 dogs for such purposes and the Allies employed similar numbers.

Many different breeds saw active duty during the war, depending on the job at hand. Bulldogs, Bloodhounds, Farm Collies, Retrievers, Dobermans, Airedales, Jack Russell and Wired Fox Terriers, Sheep Dogs and German Shepherds were all used in a variety of roles. Pure breds did not have any advantage over mixed breeds; what was important was that they displayed the proper character.

Preferred were dogs of medium build and grey or black in colour for stealth purposes, with good eyesight and a keen sense of smell. But the temperament and disposition of the dog usually came first!

Ambulance Dogs

Countless Red Cross Casualty Dogs (Ambulance Dogs) also known as Mercy Dogs took part in World War One, saving thousands of lives from both sides.

One particular dog, "Prusco", should have earned the Victoria Cross: he was said to have located and found more than one hundred wounded men after the Battle of the Somme.

Another famous ambulance dog was "Michael". The Ambulance dogs' training gave them specific skills but also encouraged them to think for themselves. The dogs were trained to bring the wounded man's cap or helmet back to the trench, and then lead medics to their fallen comrade. But often the soldier had lost his cap, or his helmet was fastened too tightly under his chin for the dog to remove it. Then the dog would have to use his initiative and pick a different item, anything that could be used to make the point: "Wounded man! Send help!"

Michael, a French Red Cross dog, made headlines with one canine decision. After a sweep of a battlefield, Michael returned, carrying the glove of a wounded soldier identified by the newspapers only as Henri. He could scarcely wait for the attendants to bring a stretcher before he started off again, his great intelligent eyes imploring them to hurry.

Michael led them to a remote part of the battlefield where they found Henri "lying still and cold." After a hasty check, they decided Henri was dead and hurried back to their trench without him.

The dog refused to accept the medics' decision and returned again and again for assistance. When he was ignored, Michael disappeared. Late that night, by the light of a full moon, a French soldier on guard duty noticed an odd movement. No more than twenty feet away, creeping slowly toward the trenches was a large dark object. The soldier had his rifle raised and was ready to shoot, but then cried out: Michael! The dog had come back with a battlefield souvenir no one could ignore. Michael was dragging Henri with parts of his uniform literally torn away by the dog's teeth. Michael, the dog, had dragged Henri, the soldier, from the battlefield, inch by inch, back to the safety of the trench. Miracle of miracles, the young soldier was breathing. Henri was whisked to a hospital, and eventually recovered.

The Germans called their dogs 'Sanitatshunde' (sanitary); equipped with their saddlebags of medical supplies, they sought out the wounded, and gave comfort to the dying. Thousands of soldiers, on both sides, owe their lives to these remarkable animals.'

Some considered the messenger dogs the real heroes of the war. These dogs were credited with indirectly saving thousands of lives by delivering vital dispatches when phone lines broke down between units at the frontline and the headquarters behind. The brave dogs faced many obstacles, such as barbed wire, slit trenches, shell holes and chemical gases.

Two of the more unusual dogs used during the Great War, were the ratters, and the YMCA cigarette dogs. Ratters were the terriers, whose natural instincts helped to keep the rat-infested muddy trenches clear; and the small Cigarette Dogs, sponsored by the YMCA, had the task of delivering cartons of cigarettes to the troops stationed on the front lines.

Soldiers of both sides adopted many dogs as mascots while fighting during World War I. Mascots, by their happy demeanour and the keen interest they showed in everything and by their readiness to respond to every kind word and to every friendly act, helped to relieve the feverish strains and stresses of war, and to keep up the morale of the men in the trenches, as it seemed nothing else on earth could do.

The famous Rin Tin Tin was actually a German messenger dog captured by the Americans. At war's end, his handler shipped him back to the USA and he became a film and television star.

Unfortunately, there were close to forty thousand dogs killed in action.

Call an Ambulance

Chapter 38

May 1917, France

Albert Miller was driving his ambulance loaded with precious cargo to the Dressing Station behind the British line at Bullecourt, France; the road was atrocious, with shell holes and deep thick mud making his progress difficult. The Germans were continuing to shell the area and the casualty list was growing exponentially.

In the back of the ambulance was his partner, Earl Petering, who was endeavouring to keep alive four badly wounded soldiers. It was not easy, as all four had severe shrapnel wounds and were bleeding profusely. One of the lads looked like he was no older than fifteen or sixteen. Earl could see the terror in his eyes: a fear of death.

The battle in and around Bullecourt was a fierce and critical one and breaking the Hindenburg Line depended on it. The Hindenburg Line was the last line of defence the Germans built in 1917. It was a mass of barbed wire, block- houses and well-constructed trenches. The village of Bullecourt sat in the middle of the line and became a fortress town. This defence line had never been penetrated and had barbed wire, in some places, one hundred metres thick. The Germans regarded it as their final fortification.

On the night of April 17th, the Australian forces attacked the Germans stationed at Bullecourt; they had no artillery and the tanks that were meant to break through the barbed wire were either broken down or had become bogged down in the snow. Major Percy Black was one of the officers leading the attack. He yelled out to his men:

       'Come on, boys, bugger the tanks!'

He charged full on, into the wire. His men leapt forward with him and fought their way into the German trenches. The Diggers were the first soldiers to break through the Hindenburg Line. Once they got through, they looked for Major Black and found him dead on the wire, his pistol still in his hand.

So many ANZACs had been killed in the attack that there were only a few left to defend the trenches. Once the Germans realized this, they mounted a counter-attack and overwhelmed the Diggers who were forced to withdraw.

The Australians returned with fresh troops three weeks later and again captured Jerry's trenches. The Germans mounted counter-attack after counter-attack for the next two weeks but finally gave up and withdrew.

The ambulance drivers, dressing stations and field hospitals were at breaking point, trying to cope with the enormous numbers of wounded soldiers. In the first Battle of Bullecourt, two thousand three hundred and thirty nine casualties were incurred from a total of three thousand Australian troops deployed.

In the Second Battle of Bullecourt, The Australians suffered ten thousand losses.

After the second battle, Albert and Earl were given three days' leave; they had earned it, working twenty hour shifts, ferrying the wounded to field hospitals.

They had become good mates and decided they would both go to Pops to enjoy their R&R.

The first stop was Talbot House where they caught up with some other drivers; there was plenty to talk about. Al and Earl then made their way up to the loft where the chapel was located and prayed not only for their own survival but the survival of the wounded from Bullecourt.

They ate in one of the many cafes in Pops and by the end of the meal both were starting to feel human again. A hotel had been arranged for them and that's where they ended up at the end of their first day. A good night's sleep is what they had been looking forward to. Ten hours later, they woke refreshed, bathed and went down to the dining room for breakfast.

They spent most of the day at Toc H playing cards with the other drivers and talking to soldiers; they even played some chess.

After their evening meal, they decided it was time for some naughty fun at "Maison de Plaisir".

Ringing the bell of this exciting establishment gave them shivers; Madame Fifi answered the door and invited the two young drivers in.

They paid Madame Fifi the required five francs and took their turn on the stairs. It was a busy night as usual; the estimated wait was one hour. There was the usual raucous laughter and continual chatter amongst the soldiers on the staircase.

The bell rang again. Madame Fifi answered, expecting another lustful soldier, but instead, a British clergyman was standing there. He pushed past her and angrily strode to the stairs.

For many months he had seen men in despair and wounded men dying from their wounds. He had been present at the two battles of Bullecourt, one of the bloodiest conflicts in the history of the war. All that was forgotten now.

Before him was a new abomination: British and Australian soldiers of all ages were lining every stair leading up to the bedrooms.

They were waiting their turn with one of the whores, in return for five francs - the equivalent of four shillings and the best part of a week's wages for the average Tommy and Digger.

'Have none of you any mothers?' he shouted furiously at the queuing men.

'Have none of you any sisters?'

Shame-faced and fearful that he might report them to their commanding officers, the men slunk out of the building, including Albert and Earl: both had mothers and sisters.

The next night, Albert and Earl were back, eager to enjoy one of the few pleasures available to them after the carnage and heartbreak they had experienced every day at the front.

Madame Fifi and One of Her Girls

Being Ernest

Chapter 39

Albert and Earl felt like new men after their R & R in Poperinge, but now it was back to the front and all the carnage that would bring.

Earl was summoned to the command centre to see his commanding officer, Major Saunderson, three days after his return.

'Private Petering, you are being transferred to another ambulance unit.'

'Yes, sir, may I ask which unit, sir?'

'The 48th Division. They have just been moved to Italy.'

'Italy, sir?'

'That's right.Italy. You leave tomorrow.

'Yes, sir, Is there anything else, sir?'

'No. That's it. You're dismissed.'

Earl returned to the ambulance station and began packing his things into his backpack; there wasn't too much to pack: spare uniform, underwear, toiletries and his book. Albert walked in.

'What in the fuck are you doing, mate? Are you fed up and decided to go home?'

'I wish. I've been posted to join the 48th in fucking Italy. I leave tomorrow.'

'Italy! I didn't even know we had a war in Italy.'

'Well, apparently we do and that's where I'm going.'

'Holy shit! How can they break up the best ambulance unit on the Western Front. I'm going to speak to old man Haig about this; it's just not on!'

'Yeah, right, give him my regards.'

Earl left at dawn to board the train which would take him to the Italian Alps.

Let's Hope They've Got a T-Bar

The trip took four days and the Tommies being transferred thought it was the break of a lifetime. They were leaving the mud and rats in the trenches of Passchendaele to fight in snow and clean crisp conditions.

Earl couldn't believe he'd be stationed so close to Venice, a city he had always dreamed of visiting. There would be no opportunity for sightseeing this trip. He knew he would be working full tilt, based on the casualty numbers he was hearing about since he arrived.

His superior officer was Captain Kennedy, a very handsome man, in a very British sort of way.

'Right, Petering, welcome aboard; you'll have your work cut for you here. We not only get the war-wounded, we also get a bloody lot of soldiers who have survived an avalanche. Mind you, not many of the poor blighters survive; they are buried in the snow, not to be found until spring.'

You'll be working with a young American volunteer - nice chap, very keen.

He's waiting to meet you in your hut so I suggest you go along and you can get acquainted.'

Earl made his way to his quarters and entered to find the American lying on his stretcher smoking a cigarette. Earl hated the smell of smoke but didn't mention it.

'Hello there. My name's Earl Petering. I believe we'll be working together.'

The American got up from his bed and shook Earl's hand.

'Please to meet you, Earl. My name's Ernest - Ernest Hemingway.'

'What brings you to be here, Ernest?

'Well, I did try to enlist in the army but the bastards rejected me on the basis my eye sight isn't so good. So I thought the next best thing would be to join the ambulance corps.'

Hemingway in his Ambulance

'What were you doing back home before you decided to join? By the way, where is home?'

'I was born in a place called Oak Park, Illinois, but I was living in Kansas City when I joined up.

'What took you to Kansas City, Ernest?'

'I was working as a reporter.'

'Really? A reporter. Sounds exciting.'

'Not really; I wrote stories about boxers, the odd shooting, nothing too exciting. The last story I wrote was about ambulance crews and the fantastic work they do. It was that story that inspired me to join up. What about you, Earl?'

242

'I was born and raised in a little village called King's Walden, Hertfordshire. Not much happened there. I was studying to be a doctor when the war broke out. Along with pretty much every other bloke in the village, I enlisted to fight for the cause, whatever that is. I suppose they thought with two years study behind me they'd whack me in the ambulance corps.'

'Are you going to finish your studies after the war, Earl?'

'I'd like to think so. I've got to live through this fucking war first.'

'Don't worry. We're ambos. Nothing happens to us.'

'I hope you're right, mate.'

On July 8, 1918, only a few weeks after arriving, fragments from an Austrian mortar shell, which had landed just a few feet away, seriously wounded Hemingway. At the time, Hemingway was distributing chocolate and cigarettes to Italian soldiers in the trenches near the front lines. The explosion knocked Hemingway unconscious, killed an Italian soldier and blew the legs off another.

Earl reported that despite over two hundred pieces of shrapnel being lodged in Hemingway's legs, he still managed to carry another wounded soldier back to the first aid station; along the way, he was hit in the legs by several machine gun bullets.

He was awarded the Italian Silver Medal for Valour, with the official Italian citation reading: "Gravely wounded by numerous pieces of shrapnel from an enemy shell, with an admirable spirit of brotherhood, before taking care of himself, he rendered generous assistance to the Italian soldiers more seriously wounded by the same explosion and did not allow himself to be carried elsewhere until after they had been evacuated."

Hemingway described his injuries to Earl when he visited him in hospital: "There was one of those big noises you sometimes hear at the front. I died then. I felt my soul or something coming right out of my body, like you'd pull a silk handkerchief out of a pocket by one corner. It flew all around and then came back and went in again and I wasn't dead any more."

Hemingway on Crutches

Italy Victorious

With a Little Help From their Friends

Chapter 40

Earl and his division had been moved to the Piave River; they sensed a major battle was looming.

The Battle of the Piave River, 1918

The Battle of the Piave River comprised the last major Austro-Hungarian attack on the Italian Front and virtually heralded the disintegration of the Austro-Hungarian army on the way to the dismantling of the empire.

The main assault was fought 15-22 June 1918; it was prompted by German demands upon their ally to launch an offensive across the Piave River. This ground was considered critical, being situated only a few kilometres from key Italian cities such as Venice and Verona. The campaign was also intended as a follow-up to the spectacularly successful combined German/Austro-Hungarian offensive at Caporetto the previous autumn.

However, the Austro-Hungarian army of June 1918 was quite different from the one that had triumphed at Caporetto eight months earlier. It was demoralised, equipment and other supplies were perilously low, and, while apparently demonstrating superior numbers of divisions to their Italian counterparts, individual unit strengths were notably weakened.

The allies, particularly America, had been for some time equipping the Italians with weapons and munitions, putting them in a position of strength.

Furthermore, incoming Chief of Staff, Armando Diaz had taken care to deploy strong defences along the Piave.

General Diaz learned the exact timing of the Austrian attack: 3:00am on June 15. At 2:30am the Italian artillery opened fire; it was an intense bombardment creating havoc along the Austrian-Hungarian front, inflicting heavy casualties. The purpose of the bombardment was to delay or stop the attack. Some Austrian soldiers began to retreat to their defensive positions, however the greater part of the Austrian force still attacked. Boroević, the Austrian Field Marshal, launched the first assault, moving south along the Adriatic Coast and the Piave River. The Austrians were able to cross the Piave and gained a bridgehead fifteen miles wide and five miles deep. The Italian army fought fiercely; Boroević was finally stopped and was forced to order a retreat. Through the following days, Boroević renewed the assault but the artillery barrage destroyed many of the river's bridges. Those Austrian formations that were able to cross the river were unable to receive reinforcement and supplies. To make matters worse, the swollen Piave River isolated a great number of units on the west bank which made them an easy target for Italian fire. An estimated twenty thousand Austro-Hungarian soldiers drowned while trying to reach the east bank. On June 19 Diaz counter-attacked and hit Boroević in the flank, inflicting heavy casualties.

Italian Soldiers

In the meantime Field Marshal Conrad attacked along the Italian lines west of Boroević on the Asiago Plateau with the objective of capturing Vicenza.

His forces gained little ground, experiencing stiff resistance by British, French and Italian units; forty thousand casualties were added to the Austrian total.

In the aftermath, Boroević was particularly critical about the tactics of Conrad who chose to continue the assaults rather than send reinforcements to the Piave sector.

With a chronic lack of supplies and facing attacks by armoured units, Emperor Karl ordered the Austro-Hungarians to retreat. He had taken personal command on June 20. By June 23, the Allies recaptured all territory on the southern bank of the Piave; the battle was over.

To the disappointment of Italy's allies, particularly Britain and France no counter-offensive followed the Battle of Piave. The Italian Army had suffered huge losses in the battle and considered a new offensive dangerous. General Armando Diaz waited for more reinforcements to arrive from the Western Front.

By October 1918, Italy finally had enough soldiers to mount an offensive. The attack targeted Vittorio Veneto, a city across the Piave. The Italian Army broke through a gap near Sacile and poured in reinforcements, crushing the Austrian defensive line. On 3 November, three hundred thousand Austrian soldiers surrendered.

Troops from Britain and France took part in this strategic offensive, losing one thousand men each.

The Battle of Vittorio Veneto heralded the dissolution of the Austro-Hungarian Army as an effective fighting force; it also triggered the disintegration of Austria-Hungary as a nation. During the last week of October, declarations made in Budapest, Prague, and Zagreb proclaimed the independence of their respective parts of the old empire. On October 29, the imperial authorities asked Italy for an armistice; the Italians refused and continued to advance, reaching Trento, Udine, and Trieste.

Villa Giusti

On 3 November, Austria-Hungary sent a flag of truce to the Italian Commander, requesting again for an armistice and terms of peace.

The Armistice with Austria was signed in the Villa Giusti, near Padua, on 3 November, and took effect on 4 November, at three o'clock in the afternoon. Austria and Hungary signed separate armistices following the overthrow of the Habsburg Monarchy and the collapse of the Austro-Hungarian Empire.

The face of Europe had changed forever.

Total Casualties, Italian Front

	Kingdom of Italy	Austro-Hungarian Empire
Killed	650,000	1,200,000
Wounded	947,000	3,620,000
POW/MIA	600,000	2,200,000

During the three-year war in the Austro-Italian Alps at least 60,000 soldiers died in avalanches.

Earl Petering and Ernest Hemingway both survived the Italian Campaign. Hemingway went on to write *A Farewell to Arms* based on his experiences in Italy. He became one of the great writers of the twentieth century. Earl returned to England, completing his medical studies and qualifying as a doctor in 1920. He progressed to become the Chief Medical Officer, the most senior medical position in the land.

Desert Storm

Chapter 41

Phillip Island, 1915

Bert Barnard was a family man, thirty years of age. He had married Anna when he was twenty-two and she was nineteen. They had two children, Anthony, aged five and Sarah, aged three. Life was good for the Barnard family; they worked a farm of two hundred acres on Phillip Island, Victoria. It was predominantly a dairy farm but they also raised pigs and a few goats.

Bert was an excellent horseman and competed in show jumping events at the various agricultural shows around Gippsland. He even came second at the Royal Melbourne Show one year.

Bert would ride into the island's township, Cowes, regularly to pick up essential supplies and go to the bank. It was on one such occasion that he stumbled across a recruitment drive for the Light Horse. Soldiers on magnificent steeds were calling for recruits to join their countrymen in Europe and fight for King and country.

It was easy to get caught up in the patriotic fever and before he knew it, he had signed up.

The hard part was going to be breaking the news to Anna. He arrived home and said nothing until the children had been put to bed.

They were sitting in front of the fire sipping their tea.

'Darling, I have some news for you; I joined up today.'

'You didn't? Tell me you're joking.'

'I'm not joking, my love. I think it is important that I make a contribution to my country.'

'What's important, *my love*, is those two children sleeping in the next room. And me for God's sake; how are we going to survive while you are away fighting some stupid war?'

'I know that Mum and Dad will lend a hand with the farm; I shouldn't be away for more than six months or so. Anyway it's done. I can't pull out now.'

Not much was said between them for the next few days. Anna started to soften her attitude eventually and the last week before Bert left for Melbourne was a happy one.

The day came; Bert kissed his wife and children and boarded the ferry, which would take him to Hastings and then by train to Melbourne.

He spent six weeks training at Broadmeadows, which was a vast tent city surrounded by thick mud.

Bert had formed some new friendships but none stronger than with William Turner; they became inseparable, even though William was born and bred in the inner suburb of Richmond. The country boy and the city lad were great mates.

The two friends caught the train bound for Albany, Western Australia, where on arrival they boarded the troop ship, *HMAS Sydney*, destination Egypt.

William was thirty-six; he and Bert were regarded as the 'elder statesmen.' They would often be asked advice on a subject or would calm heated tempers among the young soldiers.

After six weeks at sea and many bouts of sea sickness in rough weather, the Australian Light Horse 4th Division arrived in Egypt. The troops were transferred to Mena Camp about ten miles out of Cairo.

Mena Camp, Cairo, 1915

Australian Mascot

The Australians had only seen drawings of the pyramids in books at school. Most of them hadn't been more than fifty miles from their home, so seeing one of the seven wonders of the ancient world was an amazing experience.

Something else the young soldiers had not experienced was an Egyptian whore. First Battle of Wassa was the appellation given to the first of two riots in the Haret el Wassa (the brothel quarter of Cairo) involving the ANZACs (The Australian & New Zealand Army Corps). They had received news that their period of training was at an end. Orders had been received for them to embark for long--awaited action at Gallipoli.

Causes of this disturbance reportedly lay in a desire to exact revenge for past grievances arising from dealings with the district's denizens. These grievances included diluting liquor, exorbitant prices, and high rates of venereal infection. There were also rumours of stabbings of ANZAC soldiers by locals

Trouble began soon after five o'clock in the evening when soldiers began evicting whores and their pimps into the street, and tossing their possessions out after them. Bedding, furniture, clothing, even pianos, were thrown from windows of buildings several storeys high. These materials were piled in the middle of the road and set alight. Military Police from the Australian 9th Light Horse Regiment came on the scene and tried to evict the soldiers from the houses being attacked. Five arrests were made, although fellow ANZACs refused to let these men be taken away; four of the prisoners escaped.

British military police were summoned; about thirty in all, on horseback, came charging in. They were abused and showered with stones and bottles by the disgruntled soldiers. The MPs fired their pistols over the heads of the rioting crowd, wounding four. This only served to further inflame matters, and forced the police hastily to withdraw. Efforts by the Egyptian fire brigade to douse the bonfires were also frustrated. Its hose-lines were cut, its members manhandled (especially after they turned a hose onto the crowd), the engine itself was finally pushed into the flames.

The more unruly elements began to loot some shops and set fire to a Greek tavern. Shortly after seven o'clock, a second fire engine arrived, this time under cavalry escort, which exercised extreme tact, and the various fires were tackled while a still sizeable crowd looked on. The `Wassa' was close to Shepherd's Hotel, where the ANZAC commander, General Birdwood, had his headquarters, but he could do nothing to quell the riot. Eventually, armed troops were called out. After Lancashire Territorials were drawn across the road, the rioters wisely began to disperse and order was eventually restored by ten o'clock.

Burnt Out Buildings After Battle of Wassa

A formal inquiry was convened the following day under Colonel Frederic Hughes, commander of the AIF's 3rd Light Horse Brigade, to investigate the causes of the riot and establish responsibility for its outbreak. Many New Zealand officers attempted to disclaim that their men had played any part, although the evidence of their presence was quite conclusive. The Australian officers were adamant that 'New Zealanders not only took part; they predominated'.

The damages bill of £1,700 was equally shared between the Australians and New Zealanders.

A few months after the first battle of Wassa, the second battle occurred. It was very similar to the first, with many Australians and, this time, only a few New Zealanders rioting over the same gripes: prices, prostitutes and diluted alcohol.

High command stepped in and ensured there was entertainment for the troops in Cairo.

Bert and William stayed away from the riots, although they could empathise with the troops.

A popular song sung by the ANZACs was:

> *Land of heat and sweaty socks,*
> *Sin and sand and tons of pox,*
> *Streets of sorrow, streets of shame,*
> *Streets to which we give no name;*
> *Harlots, thieves and pestering wogs,*
> *Stinks and dirt and sneaking dogs,*
> *Flies that drive a man insane,*
> *Make him curse with oath profane:*

Blazing heat and aching feet,
Gyppo guts and camel meat,
Clouds of choking dust that blind,
Drive a man clean off his mind;
The Arab's heaven -- soldier's hell,
Land of Bastards, fare thee well!

In actual fact, the whores of Cairo were not beautiful women with magnificent bodies, which could lure a young soldier and seduce him with womanly charms.

> *'They tended to be a motley assortment; none of them was physically attractive. Their faces were hastily daubed with paint and powder, and the best one could say of them was that they looked the part – blowsy, all of them. One, a blonde, might have been in her early twenties; a couple of others, brunettes, would have been passable had they been properly turned out. As for the others: they were human nonentities – and very frightened.'*
> *William Turner, Trooper*

Will and Bert were given notice along with the rest of the Division; they would be moving out of camp and heading for Palestine the following day. At last they would be fighting in this war rather than hanging around Cairo trying to stay out of mischief.

The Battle of Magdhaba
Sinai, 23 December 1916

Chapter 42

At a mile distant their thousand hooves were stuttering thunder, coming at a rate that frightened a man - they were an awe inspiring sight, galloping through the red haze - knee to knee and horse to horse - the dying sun glinting on bayonet points..." Trooper Ion Idriess

The two horsemen were now ready for battle. Their horses were magnificent. Will called his 'Sultan' while Bert had chosen 'Bart'. Their commander was Major-General Harry Chauvel, an officer who led from the front. The battle in which they were about to take part was Magdhaba.

Chauvel

Magdhaba was fought on 23 December 1916 in the northern Sinai Desert, thirty-five kilometres southeast of the Mediterranean coastal town of El Arish and about thirty kilometres west of the border with Palestine.

Following their defeat at Romani, Turkish forces had no other choice other than to retreat to Bir el Abd and subsequently to Mazar. They abandoned their positions once attacked by the Australians and New Zealanders of the ANZAC Mounted Division led by Chauvel.

The objective was Palestine but before they could ride into the holy land they had to take Magdhaba and Rafa.

Magdhaba

On the night of 22 December, Chauvel was ordered to move against the inland base at Magdhaba. Riding with him was the mounted division and newly formed Imperial Camel Corps taking the place of the Brigade to which he no longer had access.

Imperial Camel Corps

Chauvel's horsemen rode in the darkness on 23 December. By daybreak, his troops had closed in on the enemy-held village. Aircraft from Number One Squadron, Australian Flying Corps, identified the Turk's positions; now Chauvel gave his orders. The Imperial Camel Corps was sent from the northwest while the horse brigades detoured around the northern flank where the firmer ground best suited horses.

The fighting was hard and intense; the ANZACs made slow progress crossing open ground under heavy fire. Soon after one o'clock, upon learning that sources of water, apart from the wells at Magdhaba, were not captured, Chauvel called off the attack. News of Chauvel's recall reached the commander of the 1st Australian Light Horse Brigade, Brigadier-General Charles Cox, just as his troops were preparing to assault the main enemy redoubt with the bayonet. He unfortunately misplaced the message until the attack was underway; his men's success showed Chauvel that victory was actually at hand.

By four o'clock that afternoon, the Turkish garrison had surrendered; few escaped. The number of enemy killed was estimated to be three hundred; thirteen hundred were captured.

The 10th Australian Light Horse Regiment, providing the blocking force south of the Wadi, accounted for seven hundred and twenty two of the prisoners. Chauvel's losses were small: one hundred and forty-six casualties, twenty-two killed. After setting fire to the village and leaving two regiments to clear the battlefield of dead and wounded, the remainder of the column returned to El Arish.

Turkish Dead

Will and Bert followed General Chauvel on to the next great adventure; the taking of Rafa, then onto Palestine.

Rafa is located on the border of Palestine; it was once an Egyptian police post.

On the 9 January, 1917, following the capture of Magdhaba, the British commander of the Desert Column, Lieutenant General Sir Philip Chetwode, prepared to take Rafa.

Aerial patrols reported there were three thousand Turks in the town, busily digging in. His troops comprised the ANZAC Mounted Division commanded by Chauvel. The Light Horse Division was reinforced by three of the four battalions of the Imperial Camel Corps comprising mainly Australians and the 5th Mounted Brigade.

After a period spent in reconnoitring routes and compiling plans of the Turkish defences from the air, Chauvel's troops commenced their march from El Arish at dusk on 8 January. They moved first to Sheikh Zowaiid, an Arab village sixteen kilometres short of the objective. Food and water was left here for both animals and men.

By dawn, the assault force had entirely surrounded Rafa and was in position to attack. However, this was not going to be easy; the Turks occupied a network of trenches rising in tiers around an earthen redoubt on a central knoll, and although these works were not protected by wire, they completely dominated the long bare slopes leading up to them.

The fighting commenced at ten o'clock; the British assault was slow. For the first time, aircraft using radio were used to direct the fire of artillery.

Things were not going that well for the Australian forces. All the reserves had already been committed and the heat was intense. Chetwode was distressed about the availability of water both for the horses and the men.

News reached him at about four o'clock that two thousand, five hundred Turkish reinforcements were approaching from the east and northeast. Chetwode decided to break off the fight and withdraw.

Acting on this order, Chauvel had issued the necessary instructions to his brigades. As at Magdhaba, the ANZACs were determined to win this fight and ignored the recall. The New Zealanders and the Australian Camel Corps both succeeded in overrunning the Turks and claimed victory. The Turkish garrison suffered two hundred killed and sixteen hundred were taken prisoner. British losses totalled four hundred and sixty, including seventy-one killed.

General Chauvel decided to retreat back to Sheikh Zowaiid where they had stored water and supplies. Fortunately the Turks did not attempt to retake the town and the troops were able to return and secure Rafa.

The next battle was Beersheba, which was a heavily fortified town forty-three kilometres from the Turkish bastion of Gaza. It anchored the right end of a defensive line that stretched from Gaza on the Mediterranean coast.

The first two frontal attacks on Gaza, in March and April 1917, failed. The British Army re-organised before attempting again. The capture of Beersheba would break the Gaza—Beersheba line and enable the British, Australian and New Zealand forces to outflank Gaza.

British attack on Beersheba

Beersheba

The twenty British Corps launched an attack on Beersheba at dawn on 31 October 1917.

By late afternoon, the corps had made little headway toward the town and its vital water wells. Lieutenant General Sir Harry Chauvel, commanding the Desert Mounted Corps, ordered the 4th Light Horse Brigade forward to attempt to secure the position.

Brigadier-General William Grant responded by ordering light horsemen of the 4th and 12th Regiments to charge at the Turkish trenches.

The light horsemen did not carry swords or lances, so they held their bayonets as their swords. The momentum of the surprise attack carried them through the Turkish defences.

The light horsemen took less than an hour to overrun the Turkish trenches and enter Beersheba.

Thirty-eight Turkish and German officers and about seven hundred other ranks were taken prisoner, and a critical supply of water was secured.

The Australians suffered sixty-seven casualties. Two officers and twenty-nine other ranks were killed. Eight officers and twenty-eight other ranks were wounded.

The fall of Beersheba opened the way to outflank the Gaza—Beersheba Line. On 6 November, after severe fighting, Turkish forces began to withdraw from Gaza, pulling back further into Palestine.

Once more, Bert and Will were in the thick of the battle and survived. They would go on to fight in a number of important battles over the coming twelve months including:

March 8–March 11 - The British capture Baghdad.

March 13-April 23 - Samarrah Offensive; British capture much of Mesopotamia.

March 26 - First Battle of Gaza. The British attempt to capture the city but fail.

October 31–November 7 - Third Battle of Gaza. The British break through the Ottoman lines.

December 8–December 26 - Battle of Jerusalem. The British enter the city (December 11)

September 19–September 25 - Battle of Megiddo. The British conquer Palestine.

The final battle was to be the taking of Damascus. Two forces were competing to be the first into this ancient city: the Australian Light Horse commanded by Chauvel and the Arabs commanded by Lawrence of Arabia; T E Lawrence.

The Race to Damascus

Chapter 43

Lawrence of Arabia

Thomas Edward (T.E.) Lawrence was born at Tremadoc in Wales in 1888. He was the son of Thomas Chapman, who later changed his surname to Lawrence after he eloped with his mistress. Thomas Lawrence was born out of marriage - a bastard, relatively rare in Victorian Britain. He was a very able pupil, though not brilliant; however, he could read at the age of four. He was also reading Latin at the age of six. Lawrence won a scholarship to Oxford University and developed a passion for reading, especially books on military history.

At Oxford University Lawrence read history and gained first class honours. While at Oxford, he travelled to the "Levant" where he visited several Crusader castles. After graduation he joined an expedition by D G Hogarth to excavate the ancient city of Carchemish in Syria. He found that he had a natural affinity with the Arab people.

He learned their language and customs and spent time reading about their history.

Wooley and Lawrence at Carchemish

When Britain declared war against Germany and her allies in August 1914, Lawrence tried to join the army. His application was refused due to his height; the minimum height set by the army was five feet five inches. However, he

269

persevered and after several months was given a commission. Lawrence joined the intelligence branch of the general staff. His knowledge of Arabic led to a posting in Egypt where he served in the 'Arab Bureau' at General Head Quarters. Lawrence stood out from the other officers who were all neat and tidy, as one would expect from a British officer: he was regarded as rather scruffy and unkempt.

The British military campaign in the Middle East had not started well. The British had easily repulsed a Turkish attack on the Suez Canal but their pursuit of the Turks across Sinai came to a halt near Gaza. The Turks had also been successful in and around Aden. The Ottoman Empire had conquered a great deal of the Middle East, which made them very unpopular with the Arabs in the region.

On June 5th, 1916, the Arab Revolt began.

The revolt had initially been successful, capturing Mecca, Jidda and Taif however the Arabs failed to capture the main rail line that ran through the region. This enabled the Turks to mobilise and transport more troops to the region, which brought the revolt to a hiatus.

In October 1916, the British Command sent Ronald Storrs and Lawrence to determine what had happened to the revolt.

Lawrence was ordered to meet with the Amir Feisal whose tribesmen had been attempting to besiege Medina. Feisal was the son of Sherif Hussein, ruler of the Hejaz.

AmirFeisal

Sherif Hussein

Feisal and Lawrence developed an immediate rapport. Feisal's men were ferocious fighters but ill-disciplined. Lawrence saw the potential of harnessing their commitment to their cause but needed strong guidance. He quickly realised that Feisal's men had little chance of capturing Medina. Lawrence knew that while the Turks controlled the rail line, they would always have the opportunity to supply their troops in Medina.

He came to the conclusion that the only effective way to defeat the Turks was to employ guerrilla warfare tactics. The rail line needed to be decommissioned. Lawrence recommended to Feisal that they leave Medina and move north.

The single-track rail line linked Medina to Damascus. He didn't want to destroy the line, as it would be needed once they defeated the Turks. His plan was to harass the Turks along the route of the rail line so that they would have to deploy more and more troops to guard it. As Lawrence and the Hejaz Arabs moved further and further north, they linked up with Trans-Jordan tribes who joined his campaign. On July 6th, 1917, Lawrence and his Arab followers captured Aqaba from the rear after defeating an entire Turkish battalion. Feisal moved his headquarters to Aqaba and placed himself and his men under the command of General Allenby, British commander in Palestine. Allenby planned to use the growing Arab revolt against the Turks to his advantage. He provided the Arabs with guns, ammunition and gold. Small numbers of British, French and Indian troops were sent to Aqaba to support Feisal's men. The Turkish Army included a number of conscripted Arab units and Allenby hoped that the success of Feisal would lead them to desert the Turkish army en masse in a demonstration of Arab unity.

As the revolt became increasingly successful, more and more Arab tribesmen joined it. This is what Allenby had hoped for. The Turks could barely cope with the revolt. On December 9th, 1917, Allenby's forces entered Jerusalem. Lawrence was with him. Both men got on with one another despite their different ranks. Allenby was quite happy for Lawrence to wear Arab dress - something other British officers could not tolerate. In January 1918, Lawrence led an attack on the Turks at Tafila in which a whole battalion was destroyed. The British had set a date for a massive attack against the Turks: September 19th, 1918. Lawrence was asked by Allenby to launch a diversionary attack on the Turks at an important rail junction at Deraa on September 17th. The attack was a great success as was Allenby's.

Feisal knew the importance to him and his people of taking Damascus. The British had promised the Arabs that they could keep any territory they conquered from the Turks. This was an integral part of the "Declaration of Seven" made by the British in Cairo a few months before.

The Arabs had a problem: the Australian Desert Mounted Corps were well ahead of them and within sight of Damascus.

The Light Horse encountered Turkish resistance and could not proceed; as the fighting grew more intense, the Australians were able to overcome the Turks and the Barada George became a sea of fleeing Turks and Germans escaping on horses, in cars and carts.

The Australians fired on the escapees, creating bedlam on the road to Damascus; the Turks encountered local Arabs who were intent on exacting vengeance for centuries of oppression.

The train was packed with Germans escaping the carnage; they were unaware that the track had been sabotaged only a few miles further down.

At ten o'clock, the Australians were ordered to bivouac for the night. The Light Horse troops were excited by the prospect of being the first to enter the great city.

The Night Before the Charge

'Hey, Bert, we showed the fucking Turks a thing or two today, didn't we mate?'

'Sure did, mate; although I think we're gunna have an even bigger day tomorrow.'

'Yeah… riding into Damascus; who would have thought?'

'Did you know anything about Damascus before the war, Will?'

'Only from what I read in the Bible. Apparently Damascus will be destroyed, leaving only rubble.'

'Geez, mate, I hope we're not gunna be responsible for that. We're meant to save the place, not fucking destroy it.'

'Na, we'll save it alright,' assured Bert.

'Come on, mate, we'd better try to get some shut eye; I think we're gunna need all our strength for tomorrow.'

The two light horsemen lay down and were soon asleep.

The air was black with thick foul-smelling smoke from the oil and ammunition dumps that had been set alight by the Turks and Germans, making it difficult to breathe.

Lawrence was also camped with the Australians, curled up next to his Rolls Royce with the gold- plated "Flying Lady" on the bonnet.

The Light Horse had received orders to block the city's exits but not to enter it. At four am they saddled up and rode towards Damascus. Their strategy was to encircle the city in a clockwise direction, preventing any Turks from leaving.

They rode towards the city's outskirts to block Homs Road to Aleppo, which was the only exit the Turks could use to escape.

The noise of the horse's hooves was deafening and the dust cloud made it almost impossible to see; it was a truly dramatic scene.

Major Olden, commander of the regiment, galloped forward, realising that encircling the city was going to be impossible. He took the decision to order the 10th Light Horse to enter the city, hoping they would not meet too much resistance. This was regarded as a very 'Australian' thing to do.

The Light Horse, with their swords drawn and their horses biting at the bit, waited for the order to charge.

'How are ya feeling, Bert?'

'Excited, scared.'

'Yeah, me too.'

'I'll be looking out for ya, mate. Don't bloody worry.'

'I know ya will, mate, me too.'

They heard the command: CHARGE.

The soldiers dug in their spurs; the horses galloped towards Damascus, manes flowing and the sound of their hooves creating a terrifying thunderous sound. The city's inhabitants could hear the rumble of the horses miles away, gradually getting louder and louder; a sound that would put terror into any enemy's heart. The speed of the charge was designed to attack the morale of the enemy and it did.

The charge created a huge dust storm making it difficult to see clearly; as they rounded a bend in the road, they encountered a group of about eight hundred infantry; they were quickly dispatched.

Australians were the first to enter Damascus

The Australians reached the barracks and discovered about twelve thousand Turks, ill equipped and some in bare feet. They had been abandoned by their commander, Mustafa Kemal, Australia's nemesis at Gallipoli. They were mostly dispirited although some yelled out 'Allah'.

As all this was happening, Lawrence, who was still miles away, was putting on the finishing touches to his wardrobe, arranging his flowing robes ready to make the grand entrance.

He hopped in the back of his Rolls Royce and headed for the great city.

Despite the speed of Lawrence's Rolls, he could not catch up with the Light Horse, who were rushing forward to Damascus, knowing full well it was likely they would be the first Europeans to take Damascus by force in over one thousand years.

The orders from High Command were clear; Feisal's Arabs accompanied by Lawrence were to be the first to enter the city. The last thing the British wanted was for the French to be the first and therefore claim Syria as theirs. The problem they had was that the Arabs were still making their way and were still some way off arriving. Lawrence hadn't been sighted since the previous evening. The orders given to the Australians were :

>*'While operating against the enemy about Damascus, care will be taken to avoid entering the town if possible. Unless forced to do so for tactical reasons, no troops are to enter Damascus. Brigadiers will arrange picquet (sic) all roads in their areas into the town to ensure this order being carried out.'*

General Allenby had wanted the surrender to be accepted by him and no one else.

He was well aware that under the terms of the Declaration of Seven, it was essential the Arabs enter first, thus ensuring a Hashemite regime would control Damascus. This would give the British some kind of control. It would also keep the French out.

The Australian Light Horse had not heard of this plan; they were riding through the ancient city with their plumed slouch hats and gleaming swords, making an impressive entrance.

Riding through the narrow streets, they came across the Hotel Victoria. Their presence had cleared the streets but in the city centre, a mass of people gathered: Arabs from various tribes in their long flowing gowns, Syrians in European dress, Jews and Greeks, even Turkish civilians welcomed the conquering heroes.

Even though the horsemen had slowed to a walk, the sound of thousands of hooves resonated off the city buildings. They were well aware that there would be caches of arms and munitions hidden in the city and kept a close watch, particularly with the residents firing off guns and rifles into the air as a sign of celebration.

Olden stopped at a very imposing building, the Serai, he dismounted and climbed the stairs, a revolver in each hand. He asked to meet with the Governor. Two solemn-looking Arabs escorted him into a large hall decorated in a very gaudy Turkish style. A small man in a large chair greeted him.

'I am here to accept your surrender,' Olden declared.

'I surrender without resistance, sir.'

At that stage, Olden was unaware that the Turks had handed power over to the Syrians before they fled.

'In the name of the City of Damascus, I welcome the first of the British Army.

Please issue a decree that there will be no more firing in the streets. It could be misinterpreted and bloodshed could occur.'

Olden rejoined his men, having declined to share a drink with the Governor; this was regarded as a gross insult to the Arabs. Olden was not to know.

The horsemen then continued to make their way through the city; this became a triumphal procession. The people were elated, clinging to the horses' necks, kissing the riders' boots and showering them with confetti and rose water.

There was no time for sight- seeing but the Light Horse knew they had travelled the same route as Saint Paul.

Where's Lawrence?

Chapter 44

Mr. Massey, writing from Damascus on October 1st, says: General Allenby's triumphant march northward into Syria this morning drive the Turks completely out of Damascus. The city was enveloped by the British, Australian, and Indian troops. The King of Hedjaz's Arab army has marched in. A few Turks who got away are scattered and demoralised. Fully 12,000 Germans and Turks were prisonered in and about the city, and a number of guns captured. The roads are shambles where the enemy resisted. Transport was smashed, and most of the material left behind was destroyed by the Germans, though some valuable transport, including a complete park of cavalry limbers, was untouched.

An hour had elapsed between the 10th Light Horse departing from the heart of Damascus and further Allied troops arriving about nine o'clock. There were many questions left unanswered: who would rule Damascus? The British? The French?

Were the Arabs going to control the city alone or were they going to be puppets of a western power?

Feisal's men had encountered the Turkish Fourth Army en route and fierce fighting broke out.

Although he was victorious, the delay could cost him the ultimate prize.

Lawrence knew that it would be preferable for the Muslims to be the first to enter the home of Islam's fourth holiest shrine, the Omayyard Mosque and the tomb of the great Muslim warrior, Saladin.

The morning was well advanced before Lawrence, wearing his dazzling white robes and curved dagger hanging from his waist, arrived in Damascus.

Celebrations had been going on for about two hours when the Allied procession through the city began.

The 14th Cavalry Brigade led them, with the French regiments attached to the 4th Australian Light Horse and the 5th Indian Division following. Lawrence was at the rear of the procession, waving the royal wave from the back seat of his open Rolls Royce.

Lawrence knew the politics of the situation better than any; he had to move quickly if Feisal was to control Damascus, however Feisal still hadn't arrived.

Over the coming years, Lawrence exerted enormous political influence over the region, not by the sword but by the pen. The Western world discovered through Lawrence's writing that the Arabs, particularly Prince Feisal and Sherif Hussein, were a significant force to be reckoned with. In his writing, he made no mention of the Australian Light Horse, instead claiming it was he, Lawrence, the conquering hero, who led the Arabs into Damascus.

He was also critical of the Australians' objectives, likening the charge to a horse race.

In turn, the Australians were critical of Lawrence and his Arab forces who committed a horrific massacre against Turkish forces at Deraa.

In essence, Lawrence hated Chauvel and was mortified that the Australian Light Horse had beaten his much-cherished Arabs into Damascus. Lawrence did not mention the Australian forces in his books or his newspaper articles. He rewrote history for his own convenience.

The fact was that the Australian Light Horse was magnificent in battle and totally dedicated. In one instance they rode fifty-eight miles in thirty-four hours, without unsaddling, to reach their objective on time.

At last, Feisal and his army arrived on 3 October from Deraa by train. They then mounted horses and galloped into Damascus. Lawrence requested Chauvel to allow Feisal and several hundred Arab warriors be permitted to stage a triumphant entry into the city: he was reluctant. However, he allowed it to go ahead. He wrote; 'As Feisal had had very little to do with the conquest of Damascus, the suggested triumphal entry did not appeal to me very much but I thought it would do no harm and gave permission accordingly.'

Feisal Enters Damascus

Lawrence wrote several inaccurate articles which were published in the *Palestine News*, stating that it was the Arabs who entered and conquered Damascus first. He well understood the power of propaganda. He then went on to author *Seven Pillars of Wisdom*, where he claimed Chauvel was subordinate to him.

Despite his faults and unbridled narcissism, Lawrence and his Arab forces fought the Turks and Germans courageously. There were no major battles like Beersheba and Haifa but they did suffer many casualties and significant hardships.

Feisal with Lawrence on his right

Lawrence Post War

Chapter 45

Lawrence accompanied the Arab delegation to the Versailles Peace Conference where it was expected that they would gain full independence for their efforts in helping the Allied war effort.

As had been the norm since time immemorial, the major powers always win. Britain and France carved up the Middle East into their own zones of influence. As a final insult to Lawrence and his Arab friend, the French evicted Feisal from Damascus. At the completion of Versailles, Lawrence resigned from the army.

He was made a Fellow of All Souls, the most prestigious award given by Oxford University, in 1919. He used his time to write *Seven Pillars of Wisdom*. Lawrence enlisted in the RAF in 1922 under the name J. M. Ross, in an effort to gain seclusion from the world of fame and glory. When the media discovered his true identity, he left the RAF and joined the Royal Tank Corps under the name T. E. Shaw. However, he did not take to this new life and rejoined the RAF in 1925. Lawrence served in India from 1927 to 1929 before returning to Britain. He stayed in the RAF until 1935.

Several months after leaving the RAF, Lawrence was engaged in his favourite passion - riding his motorbike at speed. He crashed it at 90 mph, narrowly avoiding two boys who suddenly appeared in front of him. He was only 45 years old.

Lawrence on his favourite bike

What's it all about?
Chapter 46

It's ironic that the last chapter of RED is number 42: 'the answer to life, the universe and everything'. *(The Hitchhikers' Guide to the Galaxy)*

This book is about war, greed, human endurance, love, death, comedy, cruelty and a myriad of other things, including heroism.

When doing research for this book and my other three books, I discovered a whole new world.

Total number of men mobilized to fight in World War I - 65 million

Percentage of men mobilized in World War I who died - 57 %

Total number of causalities in World War I - 37 million

Number of missing from WWI - 7.7 million

Number of wounded soldiers in WWI - 19.7 million

Number of years of fighting that took place during WWI - 4 years

Number of allied countries military causalities in WWI - 5.7 million

Number of allied civilian casualties from WWI - 3.67 million

Number of allied soldiers wounded in WWI - 12.8 million

Number of WWI Military causalities - 9,720,450

Number of Civilian casualties in WWI - 8,865,650

Total War Cost altogether of WWI - $186.3 billion

Whole cities were destroyed

Civilians executed as a lesson to others

Incredible ingenuity was employed to develop machines of war

The list goes on: this was 'the War to End all Wars'.

Yet it still goes on and on and on.

WARS FOUGHT SINCE 1900

1900-01: Boxer rebels against Russia, Britain, France, Japan, USA against rebels (35,000)

1903: Ottomans vs Macedonian rebels (20,000)

1904: Germany vs Namibia (65,000)

1904-05: Japan vs Russia (150,000)

1910-20: Mexican Revolution (250,000)

1911: Chinese Revolution (2.4 million)

1911-12: Italian-Ottoman War (20,000)

1912-13: Balkan Wars (150,000)

1915: the Ottoman Empire slaughters Armenians (1.2 million)

1915-20: the Ottoman Empire slaughters Assyrians (500,000)

1916-23: the Ottoman Empire slaughters Greek Pontians (350,000) and Anatolian Greeks (480,000)

1914-18: World War I (20 million)

1916: Kyrgyz revolt against Russia (120,000)

1917-21: Soviet Revolution (5 million)

1917-19: Greece vs Turkey (45,000)

1919-21: Poland vs Soviet Union (27,000)

1928-37: Chinese Civil War (2 million)

1931: Japanese Manchurian War (1.1 million)

1932-33: Soviet Union vs Ukraine (10 million)

1932: "La Matanza" in El Salvador (30,000)

1932-35: "Guerra del Chaco" between Bolivia and Paraguay (117.500)

1934: Mao's Long March (170,000)

1936: Italy's invasion of Ethiopia (200,000)

1936-37: Stalin's purges (13 million)

1936-39: Spanish Civil War (600,000)

1937-45: Japanese invasion of China (500,000)

1939-45: World War II (55 million) including Holocaust and Chinese Revolution

1946-49: Chinese Civil War (1.2 million)

1946-49: Greek Civil War (50,000)

1946-54: France-Vietnam War (600,000)

1947: Partition of India and Pakistan (1 million)

1947: Taiwan's uprising against the Kuomintang (30,000)

1948-1958: Colombian Civil War (250,000)

1948-1973: Arab-Israeli wars (70,000)

1949-: Indian Muslims vs Hindus (20,000)

1949-50: Mainland China vs Tibet (1,200,000)

1950-53: Korean War (3 million)

1952-59: Kenya's Mau Mau insurrection (20,000)

1954-62: French-Algerian War (368,000)

1958-61: Mao's "Great Leap Forward" (38 million)

1960-90: South Africa vs Africa National Congress (unknown)

1960-96: Guatemala's Civil War (200,000)

1961-98: Indonesia vs West Papua/Irian (100,000)

1961-2003: Kurds vs Iraq (180,000)

1962-75: Mozambique Frelimo vs Portugal (10,000)

1962-75: Angolan FNLA & MPLA vs Portugal (50,000)

1964-73: USA-Vietnam War (3 million)

1965: second India-Pakistan War over Kashmir

1965-66: Indonesian Civil War (250,000)

1966-69: Mao's "Cultural Revolution" (11 million)

1966-: Colombia's Civil War (31,000)

1967-70: Nigeria-Biafra Civil War (800,000)

1968-80: Rhodesia's Civil War (unknown)

1969-: Philippines vs the communist Bagong Hukbong Bayan/ New People's Army (40,000)

1969-79: Idi Amin, Uganda (300,000)

1969-02: IRA - Northern Ireland's Civil War (3,000)

1969-79: Francisco Macias Nguema, Equatorial Guinea (50,000)

1971: Pakistan-Bangladesh Civil War (500,000)

1972-: Philippines vs Muslim separatists (Moro Islamic Liberation Front, etc) (150,000)

1972: Burundi's Civil War (300,000)

1972-79: Rhodesia/Zimbabwe's Civil War (30,000)

1974-91: Ethiopian Civil War (1,000,000)

1975-78: Menghitsu, Ethiopia (1.5 million)

1975-79: Khmer Rouge, Cambodia (1.7 million)

1975-89: Boat people, Vietnam (250,000)

1975-87: Civil War in Lebanon (130,000)

1975-87: Laos' Civil War (184,000)

1975-2002: Angolan Civil War (500,000)

1976-83: Argentina's military regime (20,000)

1976-93: Mozambique's Civil War (900,000)

1976-98: Indonesia-East Timor Civil War (600,000)

1976-2005: Indonesia-Aceh (GAM) Civil War (12,000)

1977-92: El Salvador's Civil War (75,000)

1979: Vietnam-China War (30,000)

1979-88: the Soviet Union invades Afghanistan (1.3 million)

1980-88: Iraq-Iran War (435,000)

1980-92: Sendero Luminoso - Peru's Civil War (69,000)

1984-: Kurds vs Turkey (35,000)

1981-90: Nicaragua vs Contras (60,000)

1982-90: Hissene Habre, Chad (40,000)

1983-: Sri Lanka's Civil War (70,000)

1983-2002: Sudanese Civil War (2 million)

1986-: Indian Kashmir's Civil War (60,000)

1987-: Palestinian Intifada (4,500)

1988-2001: Afghanistan Civil War (400,000)

1988-2004: Somalia's Civil War (550,000)

1989-: Liberian Civil War (220,000)

1989-: Uganda vs Lord's Resistance Army (30,000)

1991: Gulf War - large coalition against Iraq to liberate Kuwait (85,000)

1991-97: Congo's Civil War (800,000)

1991-2000: Sierra Leone's Civil War (200,000)

1991-2009: Russia-Chechnya Civil War (200,000)

1991-94: Armenia-Azerbaijan War (35,000)

1992-96: Tajikstan's Civil War (50,000)

1992-96: Yugoslavian Wars (260,000)

1992-99: Algerian Civil War (150,000)

1993-97: Congo Brazzaville's Civil War (100,000)

1993-2005: Burundi's Civil War (200,000)

1994: Rwanda's Civil War (900,000)

1995-: Pakistani Sunnis vs Shiites (1,300)

1995-: Maoist rebellion in Nepal (12,000)

1998-: Congo/Zaire's War - Rwanda and Uganda vs Zimbabwe, Angola and Namibia (3.8 million)

1998-2000: Ethiopia-Eritrea War (75,000)

1999: Kosovo's Liberation War - NATO vs Serbia (2,000)

2001-: Afghanistan's Liberation War - USA & UK vs Taliban (40,000)

2002-: Cote d'Ivoire's Civil War (1,000)

2003-11: Second Iraq-USA War - USA, UK and Australia vs Saddam Hussein and subsequent Civil War (160,000)

2003-09: Sudan vs JEM/Darfur (300,000)

2004-: Sudan vs SPLM & Eritrea (unknown)

2004-: Yemen vs Shiite Muslims (unknown)

2004-: Thailand vs Muslim separatists (3,700)

2007-: Pakistan vs Pakistani Taliban (38,000)

2012-: Iraq's Civil War after the withdrawal of the USA (unknown)

2012-: Syria's Civil War (70,000 and continuing)

Arab-Israeli Wars

I (1947-49): Israeli (6,373) and Arabs (15,000) die

II (1956): Israeli (231) and Egyptians (3,000) die

III (1967): Israeli (776) and Arabs (20,000) die

IV (1973): Israeli (2,688) and Arabs (18,000) die

Intifada I (1987-92): Israelis (170) and Palestinians (1,000)

Intifada II (2000-03): Israelis (700) and Palestinians (2,000)

Israel-Hamas war (2008): Palestinians (1,300)

Approximately 265,000,000 people have died from wars since the beginning of the twentieth century.

War Quotes:

Every gun that is made, every warship launched, every rocket fired, signifies in the final sense a theft from those who hunger and are not fed, those who are cold and are not clothed.
(Dwight D. Eisenhower)

The object of war is not to die for your country but to make the other bastard die for his.
(George S. Patton)

Never think that war, no matter how necessary, nor how justified, is not a crime.
(Ernest Hemingway)

What is human warfare but just this; an effort to make the laws of God and nature take sides with one party.
(Henry David Thoreau)

All war is deception.
(Sun Tzu)

There is no instance of a nation benefiting from prolonged warfare.
(Sun Tzu)

In modern war... you will die like a dog for no good reason.
(Ernest Hemingway)

If we don't end war, war will end us. (H. G. Wells)

A soldier will fight long and hard for a bit of coloured ribbon.
(Napoleon Bonaparte)

There is no avoiding war; it can only be postponed to the advantage of others.
(Niccolo Machiavelli)

War grows out of the desire of the individual to gain advantage at the expense of his fellow man.
(Napoleon Hill)

In peace, sons bury their fathers. In war, fathers bury their sons.
(Herodotus)

Patriots always talk of dying for their country and never of killing for their country.

(Bertrand Russell)

All wars are civil wars, because all men are brothers.

(Francois Fenelon)

To walk through the ruined cities of Germany is to feel an actual doubt about the continuity of civilization.

(George Orwell)

The military don't start wars. Politicians start wars.

(William Westmoreland)

An unjust peace is better than a just war.

(Marcus Tullius Cicero)

Older men declare war. But it is the youth that must fight and die.

(Herbert Hoover)

One may know how to gain a victory, and know not how to use it.

(Pedro Calderon de la Barca)

The direct use of force is such a poor solution to any problem; it is generally employed only by small children and large nations.

(David Friedman)

War is a series of catastrophes, which result in victory.

(Albert Pike)

War would end if the dead could return.

(Stanley Baldwin)

I know not with what weapons World War III will be fought, but World War IV will be fought with sticks and stones.

(Albert Einstein)

A Poem by Siegfried Sassoon

"The rank stench of those bodies haunts me still"

The rank stench of those bodies haunts me still
And I remember things I'd best forget.
For now we've marched to a green, trenchless land
Twelve miles from battering guns: along the grass

Brown lines of tents are hives for snoring men;

Wide, radiant water sways the floating sky

Below dark, shivering trees. And living-clean

Comes back with thoughts of home and hours of sleep.

To-night I smell the battle; miles away

Gun-thunder leaps and thuds along the ridge;

The spouting shells dig pits in fields of death,

And wounded men, are moaning in the woods.

If any friend be there whom I have loved,

God speed him safe to England with a gash.

It's sundown in the camp; some youngster laughs,

Lifting his mug and drinking health to all

Who come unscathed from that unpitying waste:

(Terror and ruin lurk behind his gaze.)

Another sits with tranquil, musing face,

Puffing his pipe and dreaming of the girl

Whose last scrawled letter lies upon his knee.

The sunlight falls, low-ruddy from the west,

upon their heads. Last week they might have died

And now they stretch their limbs in tired content.

One says 'The bloody Bosche has got the knock';

'And soon they'll crumple up and chuck their games.

'We've got the beggars on the run at last!'

Then I remembered someone that I'd seen

Dead in a squalid, miserable ditch,

Heedless of toiling feet that trod him down.

He was a Prussian with a decent face,

Young, fresh, and pleasant, so I dare to say.

No doubt he loathed the war and longed for peace,

And cursed our souls because we'd killed his friends.

One night he yawned along a half-dug trench

Midnight; and then the British guns began

With heavy shrapnel bursting low, and 'hows'

Whistling to cut the wire with blinding din.

He didn't move; the digging still went on;

Men stooped and shovelled; someone gave a grunt,

And moaned and died with agony in the sludge.

Then the long hiss of shells lifted and stopped.

He stared into the gloom; a rocket curved,

And rifles rattled angrily on the left

Down by the wood, and there was noise of bombs.

Then the damned English loomed in scrambling haste

Out of the dark and struggled through the wire,

And there were shouts and curses; someone screamed

And men began to blunder down the trench

without their rifles. It was time to go:

He grabbed his coat; stood up, gulping some bread;

Then clutched his head and fell.

I found him there

In the grey morning when the place was held.

His face was in the mud; one arm flung out

As when he crumpled up; his sturdy legs

Were bent beneath his trunk; heels to the sky.

Siegfried Sassoon

The End

Bibliography

http://www.awm.gov.au/encyclopedia/enlistment/ww1/

http://www.dailymail.co.uk/femail/article-1065433/Sex-Somme-How-British-soldiers-solace-arms-local-girls.html

http://www.historicroadways.co.uk/destination-western-front.html

http://users.telenet.be/aandeschreve/ginger.htm

http://www.westernfrontonline.net/features/article_eb36889c-0a0b-5855-956f-d5714aac099f.html

http://www.ww1battlefields.co.uk/flanders/pop.html

http://www.heretical.com/costello/14govert.html

http://www.oldmagazinearticles.com/World_War_One_Animals

http://www.historylearningsite.co.uk/poperinge_world_war_one.htm

http://www.historylearningsite.co.uk/malmedy_massacre.htm

http://europeanhistory.about.com/cs/worldwar1/a/blww1casualties.htm

http://www.oldmagazinearticles.com/WW1_carrier-pigeons_information_pdf

http://www.kellscraft.com/MountainPaths/MountainPathsCh06.html

https://en.wikipedia.org/wiki/Italian_Front_(World_War_I)

http://www.worldwar1.com/itafront/avalan.htm

http://www.history.com/this-day-in-history/ernest-hemingway-wounded-on-the-italian-front

http://www.1914-1918.net/italy.htm

https://en.wikipedia.org/wiki/T._E._Lawrence

http://en.wikipedia.org/wiki/Arab_Revolt

http://www.jill-hamilton.com/first-to-damascus.html

Acknowledgements

Thankyou to my wife Anna for tolerating my obsession

Thankyou to David Needum, Kim Krarup and Chris M McIntyre for reading the manuscript and giving their opinions and approvals.

Thankyou Desma Pacitto for another great cover.

Thankyou Janet Upcher for another great edit.

Copyright